Milly stared blankly at JD. "A demon?"

He nodded.

"A demon?" she said again.

"Yes," JD said. "Demon."

"Come on. Is this like some weird reality TV show?"

"No, fighting demons is our job."

"Fighting demons? Running around with swords?"
She gestured at the weapon in JD's hands. "But you're
a...a boy band."

SLAY

KIM CURRAN

USBORNE

To Amy,
Conqueror of mountains.

This edition first published in the UK in 2018 by Usborne Publishing Ltd.,
Usborne House, 83-85 Saffron Hill, London EC1N 8RT, England. www.usborne.com

Copyright © Kim Curran, 2018.

The right of Kim Curran to be identified as the author of this work has been asserted by
her in accordance with the Copyright, Designs and Patents Act, 1988.

The name Usborne and the devices ♀ 🎈 USBORNE are Trade Marks of
Usborne Publishing Ltd.

A CIP catalogue record for this book is available from the British Library.

J MAMJJASOND/18 04417/1 ISBN 9781474932318

Printed in the UK

The road keeps on callin'

"Thank you, Illinois!"

With a last strum of guitar and an explosion of lights, the show ended. Thousands of voices called out for more. Girls screamed, sobbing and broken-hearted, wanting the show to go on for ever. Boys cried out too, wanting to hear another of their favourite songs. But the show had to end.

JD scanned the audience one last time. Thousands of faces illuminated by the glowing screens of phones gazed back at him. The face he was looking for wasn't there. It never was.

He waved, then followed the rest of the boys offstage. The huge Slay logo lit his way, not that he needed it. He'd know his way through the viper's nest of black cables with his eyes closed.

Gail, the band's manager, watched from the wings, her hands folded over the silver tip of her cane. "Now *that*, JD," she said as he approached, her diamond-encrusted eyepatch flashing as bright as her one dark eye, "is what I meant about making a connection. Could you feel it?" She gripped his shoulder and gave him a small shake.

It was almost annoying how Gail was always right about these things. She'd gone on and on about how he had to open himself up to the audience. Be vulnerable. Be exposed. Something JD didn't do with people he'd known for years, let alone with thousands of strangers. But tonight, something had happened. He'd let his guard down and the crowd in. Their love had poured into him, filling a hole in his soul he'd never realized was there.

"Yeah," he said with a half shrug. "It was kinda cool."

"Kinda cool? You muppet," Tom said, jumping on JD's shoulders. Tom was the only one who could insult JD without getting at least a punch on the arm for it. He smiled, his round cheeks, which had whole forum threads dedicated to them, creasing beneath sparkling green eyes. Tom was a few months older than JD, but you wouldn't know it to look at him. "*Cute*" and "*baby-faced*" were used to describe Tom in almost every article about the band, much to his irritation. But it was true. That bundle of strawberry-blond curls with that fresh, freckled face made Tom look angelically youthful. "It was more than 'kinda cool', it was amazing!"

"You know what was amazing?" JD said. "That sweet keyboard solo on 'Bring It Home'. Where did that come from?"

Tom turned his palms up to the sky. "What can I say, I'm a natural talent."

"A natural something." JD wrapped his arm around his bandmate's neck and knuckled his hair, which he knew would annoy their stylist. But he didn't care. The show was over for tonight. He and Tom jostled each other as they headed down the stairs backstage, laughing and revelling in the post-show high.

Connor jumped around, whooping and drumming his sticks off everything in sight. He was like a living, breathing wind-up toy. JD wondered if the day would come when Connor would run out of energy. He'd known him for two years now and there was no sign of it yet. Connor grabbed a can of cola off a passing roadie and shook it before opening it.

"Watch the threads!" Zek dodged the spray of liquid and checked his clothes for any stains. They were, as ever, impeccable. Everything about the band's bassist was sharp. Including his tongue. "Which reminds me, Con, a scarecrow called earlier, he wants his trousers back," Zek said, returning to his phone to put the finishing touches to his post.

Zek was constantly documenting their lives on social media. Well, some of their lives. Slay got up to so many things that the public could never, ever know about.

Connor drained the can in one long gulp, crushed it and threw it at Zek. Zek snatched it out of the air one-handed without even looking up from his phone.

"Show-off," Connor muttered.

"You know the difference between a drummer and a drum machine?" Zek said. "You only have to punch the information into a drum machine once."

Niv stretched out his slender hands and slapped both his twin and Connor around the back of the head, knocking Connor's cap to the floor and making both boys laugh.

Always the peacekeeper, JD thought. Niv didn't need to say a word to bring an end to Connor and Zek's frequent squabbles. A look was normally enough. Unlike his twin brother, who never shut up, Niv hadn't spoken a single word in over eight years, not since their parents had tragically died. His angular face was uniquely expressive though: with the raise of an eyebrow or the twist of his mouth, Niv could speak volumes.

JD looked around the band, the familiar glow of respect and warmth filling him. That had been a show to remember. The five boys had been more in sync than ever before. Zek on bass and Connor on drums laying down tight rhythms that allowed Niv on guitar and Tom on keyboards to play it loose. And all the time, JD sang his heart out.

They were coming to the end of their first world tour after nearly five months on the road. And while JD couldn't deny the kick he got out of playing to packed stadiums, he loved these smaller gigs the most. They'd played a lot of surprise shows at venues like tonight's: a run-down baseball field in a middle-of-nowhere town, announced last-minute on social media. It was one of their *things*. The media thought it was a gimmick, orchestrated to build hype – never knowing where the next Slay gig would be until a day before kept the fans speculating wildly online. The fans themselves loved it. They thought it was all because the boys wanted to give something back, that it was proof of how much Slay cared about them. And they were right. But for the wrong reasons.

"Er, 'scuse me, JD." One of their roadies waited at the bottom of the stairs, twisting a small leather cap in his huge tattooed hands.

"Hey, Carl," JD said. The roadie's bearded face lit up at the lead singer knowing his name. JD didn't have the heart to tell him he knew it only because the man had *Carl loves Betty* tattooed across his arm.

"I'm sorry to bother you, only…" The giant man stepped aside, revealing a small blonde girl standing behind him. She wore a miniature version of Carl's leather jacket and, under it, a Slay T-shirt. "This is my daughter, Daisy, and she really wanted to meet you."

The girl's eyes were the size of ping-pong balls and she shook in her mini biker boots. She couldn't have been much older than eight.

JD kneeled down and stretched out his hand. "It's a pleasure to meet you, Daisy." The girl held up a tiny hand and JD shook it. "Did you enjoy the show?"

Daisy nodded frantically and said in a wobbling voice,

"It was the best…night…of my life."

"Can I let you in on a secret?" JD said. He looked left and right, then beckoned the little girl forward with a finger and whispered in her ear. "It was one of the best nights of my life too."

The girl's smile was so big JD worried it might split her face in half. He straightened up and gave her a gentle half hug. The emotion was too much. Tears started flowing and she buried her face in her father's leg, bawling.

Carl scooped his daughter up. "I haven't seen her this happy since before we lost her mum," he said, casting a meaningful look at JD.

JD knew what losing someone was like. Everyone in Slay did, from the band to the roadies. It was why they had been chosen. "Take care of each other."

Carl muttered his thanks and carried the girl away.

"What is it with you and making girls cry?" Tom said.

"It's his face," Zek said, without looking up from his phone. "It makes everyone cry. Kids. Old ladies. That statue in New Orleans."

"Ah, now, that was a miracle," Connor said, tapping his forehead, chest and shoulders with the tip of his drumstick to make the sign of the cross.

"You're not joking," Zek said, holding his phone up and snapping a picture of JD. "A face that ugly? Doesn't happen by accident."

"Don't post that!" JD said.

"Too late. Oh and look, twenty views already."

JD punched Zek playfully on the arm. Some days Zek's endless attempts to wind him up worked, but not today.

Connor slammed open the dressing-room door with a scissor kick and they all piled in. Gail closed the door behind them, locking the publicists and stylists, journalists and bloggers out on the other side.

JD inhaled deeply, taking in the smell of the room. The chemical tang of hairspray and aftershave still lingered from when they were primped before going onstage. And there was the sweet waft of the warm pizzas cooling in the corner – the only rider the boys asked for.

Gail propped herself up on the dressing table, leaning her silver-tipped cane against the wall, and reached out her arms. Her mass of bracelets jangled. "My boys. My brilliant boys." A tear glistened in the corner of her heavily-kohled eye, out of character for the usually no-nonsense woman. But then it had been a long week.

The five huddled together, their arms reaching around each other's shoulders, their heads bowed. They always gave thanks after every show. Connor and the twins to their separate gods, Tom and JD to fate or destiny or whatever had brought them together. JD didn't know what Gail gave thanks for, but he sure gave thanks for her.

She'd been a lead singer herself, so she knew the pressure

and privilege that came with being the frontman. Her band – a British all-girl rock band called The Cyclones – were at the height of their global success when there had been a tragic accident. Gail had been the sole survivor, and she still bore the scars: a shattered leg and a missing eye. And they were only the physical ones.

"A performance like that after what happened in Nebraska," Gail said. "I'm so proud. However…" She straightened up and broke the circle as the boys groaned. They knew what that *However* meant. "It's back to business." She clapped her hands together.

Connor rolled his eyes. "Sure, can't we have one night off? There's this deadly fairground on the other side of town."

"Wait! You don't mean where spooky old man Jones lives?" Zek said in a fake eerie voice.

"And I would have gotten away with it too, if it wasn't for you meddling kids!" Tom added, his creepy-old-man voice somewhat ruined by a mouthful of pizza. "Come to think of it," he said, swallowing and dropping back into his soft London accent, "we *are* just like the Scooby-Doo gang!"

"Yes, and Connor is Shaggy," Zek said, and the rest of the boys hooted in agreement.

"Yeah, yeah. Laugh it up," Connor said, spinning his snapback cap around on his messy hair. "Anyway, how do you even know about Scooby-Doo?"

Zek gazed dramatically into the far distance. "When Niv

and I were small children growing up in the mountains outside of Marrakech an old storyteller would come to our village and re-enact the great tales of the Mystery Gang and their battle against the forces of evil. We didn't have any dogs so the role of Scooby-Doo was played by a goat."

Niv wiped away a fake tear.

"Good days," Zek said, resting his hand on his brother's shoulder. "Happy days."

Connor stood open-mouthed. "For real?"

Zek and Tom burst out laughing. Connor was sweet and a great drummer, but he was such a sucker.

JD took pity on him. "They have cable TV in Morocco you know, Connor?"

Connor blinked, taking a full minute before he got the joke. He threw his sticks at Zek's head. "Shove off the lot of ya. Sure, I knew you were having me on. I knew."

Niv hooked a finger in his mouth, like a fish caught on a line, and dangled his tongue out.

"And you can shut your gob too, Niv," Connor said, shoving the bassist.

Gail pulled Connor off Niv. "Maybe we can go see who's haunting the fairground tomorrow. After your radio interview with Jack Caroll."

JD groaned. He sucked at interviews. He never knew what to say and always managed to put his foot in it. "Do I have to?"

"Yes," Gail said. "It's all part of the job, boys. But…" She smiled. "You know what else is part of the job?"

JD grinned in anticipation. They hadn't come to Illinois just to play a gig. "Sending unwelcome visitors back to hell?"

Gail nodded. "We've tracked three black-eyed scumbags to a motel just outside of town. So, tool up."

The boys cheered. Slay did two things. And they did them well. Play killer music and kick demon butt.

Music done. It was butt-kicking time.

Home is where you are

"Hello," Milly shouted, closing the door behind her, "I'm home."

There was no response, as usual. The house was empty and she was alone. Again. She swung her bag off her shoulder and dropped it to the floor, then kicked off her thick-heeled shoes and threw her purple school blazer at the foot of the metal coat stand. Petty victories. Especially as she knew she'd pick them all up before the housekeeper arrived in the morning.

The house was too big. Too quiet. They'd moved to Chicago less than a month ago and into this tumbling-down mansion on the edge of the city. Milly had become accustomed to living in stylish penthouse apartments, all huge glass windows and sharp modern art, but her mother's new agent had been quite insistent about this house, telling her that it was best she have somewhere quiet and out of the way. Given he was the one who'd got her the deal with the Lyric Opera of Chicago after everything had gone so wrong with the English National Opera, Milly thought she should at least try and be grateful. Not easy, considering she hated the man almost as much as she'd hated leaving London. She'd tried to argue about the move. Lied about how settled she was in her school to avoid the pain of yet more upheaval. But none of that mattered to her mother.

"It will be magnificent, *ma chérie*. Another adventure!"

Sure, another adventure for you, Milly had thought at the time. *But more boredom for me.*

She'd spent her entire life being dragged from city to city as her mother's career as an opera singer rose and then fell. From prima donna at the Opéra de Paris to chorus at the English National Opera, via Berlin and Sydney. And now a role at the Lyric Opera in Chicago. Milly's only hope had been that she'd finally be able to go to a normal school. The kind she'd seen on US TV shows: all jocks and cheerleaders and shining teeth. But yet again she'd been sent to the most expensive, most uptight, most boring school in the area.

Milly longed for an adventure of her own, one where she got to be the hero of her own life. But for now she was still just a background character in her mother's epic story.

She slouched into the living room and fired up the TV. Flicking through the channels, she stopped on a pop concert of five boys playing to a crowd of screaming fans. Milly smiled guiltily. She had been expressly instructed not to listen to music like this. "It will rot your brain," her mother had said, before proceeding to shake the windows with her vocal exercises. *Officially* she had been forbidden from watching TV too, unless it was to help with her studies. But she was sixteen now – time to start breaking some of her mother's rules. Especially if her mother wasn't around to see her breaking them. She turned the sound up.

The music didn't sound like it could do her brain any damage. It was catchy – she even heard echoes of Rossini's *The Thieving Magpie* in the chorus. And the boys were undeniably easy on the eyes. She recognized them from pictures stuck to the insides of lockers and plastered over folders at school. The lead singer had the most intense grey eyes that seemed to look only at her. And the boy on keyboards had a smile that seemed to light up the whole stage. The rest of the band was made up of a pair of twins on guitars, with light brown skin and golden eyes, and a mop-haired drummer, who was all muscles and freckles. She was starting to understand why her classmates had been so excited when they'd heard the band were coming to Illinois.

"What if we, like, actually get to meet them?" one of the girls had squealed. "And they invite us backstage? Imagine!"

"What if they ask us to come on tour?" another replied. "Imagine!"

The girls at school liked to imagine a lot of things when

it came to boy bands. Yet another way Milly felt like an outsider.

She turned off the TV and slouched into the kitchen. Not even so much as a note from her mother. Between rehearsals and five shows a week, Milly had hardly seen her since they'd arrived. Although it was better than the weeks after her mother had been fired from the ENO and spent all day at home, wailing as only a soprano can. No, Milly was happy her mother had got this new job, but it did mean she'd have to make her own dinner, again. She opened the fridge and considered the contents. Five cabbages and a bag of lemons. Her mother was on a cleansing diet.

"Yummy."

She slammed the fridge door in disgust and popped two slices of white bread into the silver toaster. They bounced back up exactly three minutes and twenty-six seconds later, as the toaster had been programmed, and she grabbed them out of the air. After slathering them with peanut butter, she shoved one slice into her mouth and carried the other with her into the music room, her favourite room in the house.

While the rest of the house was big and rambling, the music room was small and cosy, and the only one with a view of Lake Michigan.

She licked her fingers clean of peanut butter and wiped her hands on her scratchy, tartan school skirt twice – three times to be sure – before opening the lid of the Steinway piano. She splayed her hands on the off-white keys, stretching out her thumbs and little fingers as far as she could, and pressed down, drinking in the sound of her favourite chord: B flat.

She had Latin homework to do tonight. An advanced physics paper to check after that. But for now, all Milly wanted to do was play.

She sat on the green leather stool, shuffled it closer to the piano till it was in the perfect position, then let her fingers dance. She moved seamlessly from Bach to Rachmaninov, onto a blues piece she'd been trying to master, then onto a song of her own composition – which, she wasn't going to admit to anyone, she loved even more than the others.

Milly was, she'd overheard her mother saying once, "good at everything". From some mothers, that would have been meant as a compliment. From Milly's mother, it was a comment on how her daughter lacked focus. But the truth was Milly did have a focus: music. It was the only thing that came naturally to her. The rest – the maths, physics, languages – she had to work at. And work hard. But not music. If she'd had her way, she would have done nothing but play the piano 24/7. But her mother wouldn't allow that.

"You do not have *la constitution* for a life in music, *ma trésor*. You are too gentle. Too like your dear papa." And she would cross herself and change the subject.

So Milly focused on her studies, ready to sit her exams and then go to the Sorbonne in Paris, like her mother wanted. She was nothing if not a dutiful daughter.

Her father had been gentle, about that her mother was right. A kind British-Chinese man, with a smile as big as his heart. He and her mother had always looked a little ridiculous standing next to each other. Her curvaceous mother, larger – and louder – than life. Her father small and silent. The fact that he was deaf had been a subject of much amusement to everyone who knew the couple. Some even thought it might have been the secret to their successful marriage. Others, Milly heard via whispers behind her mother's back, put it down to his extreme wealth.

Her father had bought Milly her first piano and would sit with her while she played, feeling the vibrations through his hands and feet and telling her how well she was doing. He had died of cancer three years ago and she missed him more than her heart could take sometimes. Every time she sat down to play, she would imagine him there, sitting next to her, his hand on the piano, nodding encouragingly.

As she played, the ache in her shoulders lessened and the tension of the day flowed out of her and into the piano. All the worry about exams and the snide comments of her new schoolmates fell away. At times like this, she didn't know where the piano ended and she began.

She was so lost in the music that she didn't notice the

three people standing in the doorway, watching. As Milly played the last chord, pressing down on the sustain pedal to draw it out, they started to clap.

She jumped at the sound, nearly falling off the stool. "*Maman!* You almost gave me a heart attack."

"*Bravo*," her mother said, eyes shining.

Her mother seemed to fill every room she was in – even after she'd left them. Or maybe it was just her perfume: a sweet musk that clung to everything and everyone in her wake.

"I didn't realize your daughter was quite so talented," the man next to her said. This was her mother's new American manager who, to Milly's annoyance, went by his surname only: Mourdant. He wore sharp, silver suits and sunglasses indoors, and Milly hated him with an intense passion she reserved only for politicians and people who were mean to dogs. Milly was almost certain something was going on between the two of them. The way her mother looked at him like he was a god made her skin crawl.

The other person was her mother's new personal assistant. April? Alice? Milly hadn't bothered to remember her name because her mother's PAs never stayed around too long. This one looked just like all the others. Small, dark and birdlike. Although maybe all women looked like that in her mother's presence.

"Yes, very beautiful, Milly," Alice/April said.

"Pff! The child's name is Lyudmila! How many times do I have to tell you, Alice?"

"Yes, sorry, Madam Durand."

Her mother never called her Milly. Only ever her full name – Lyudmila – after her first starring role.

"We didn't expect you to be home," Mourdant said.

Milly closed the lid of the piano, uncomfortable under the man's intense gaze.

"Um…where did you think I'd be?"

"School or something." He waved his hand around, showing his complete lack of interest in whatever that something might be.

"School finished, like, five hours ago."

"The library then?" He said everything through a thick smile of blindingly white teeth and yet there was never any warmth. Every time Milly looked at him, she thought of sharks.

"The librarian kicked me out so she could lock up. So, um, sorry, I'm right here, like always. It's you I didn't expect to be around."

"We're celebrating."

"Celebrating what?" Milly asked.

Mourdant reached into his jacket and Milly saw a flash of crimson lining. He pulled out a fold of cream paper. "Your mother is about to sign a new contract!" With a flick of his hand, the paperwork unrolled.

"With the opera house? I thought you were already employed by them," Milly said. *After all*, she thought, *it's the reason you dragged me here.*

"This is for something new. Something…life-changing." He folded the contract back up, returned it to his jacket pocket, and looked at Milly's mother. "Isn't that right, Isobel?"

Milly's mother gazed up at Mourdant, her eyes glittering like an infatuated teenager's. "Yes, life-changing."

"Congratulations, I guess," Milly said after a moment, wanting to break the awkward silence.

It seemed to shatter whatever trance her mother was in. "Yes, we must celebrate. But first, come here and give your mother a kiss."

Milly pushed the stool away and walked stiffly over to her mother. She offered her cheek, ready to receive her mother's usual cold double kiss – but instead she was scooped up into a hug and pressed against her mother's substantial bosom so hard she could barely breathe.

"*Maman*…you're crushing me."

"Everything is going to change, *ma chérie*," she breathed into Milly's ear. "We're going to have everything we ever dreamed of."

Milly pushed herself free of the embrace. Her shock was quickly replaced by a creeping uneasiness. Her mother was acting so weird. So…loving. She should probably be concerned – but it was actually freaking her out a little.

23

"I've, um, got to…homework," Milly mumbled and headed for the stairs.

"I am going to cook for us all to celebrate, won't that be nice?"

"I'm not hungry."

"Then why don't you join us later for a glass of champagne to toast your mother's success," Mourdant said. It wasn't a question.

"Oh, yes, your first taste of champagne! Won't that be fun?"

Milly had to grip the banister to stop herself from falling over. She looked back at her mother smiling up at her, Mourdant by her side.

"Sure," Milly said, a cold shiver creeping up her spine, before racing up the steps two at a time.

Once inside her room, she closed the door, locked it and leaned against it. Her mother never cooked. Not once in her life. She had people do it for her. And "*fun*"? Her mother never wanted her to have fun.

Milly didn't know what was happening. But she knew one thing. Something very, very weird was going on.

While you sleep

"You sure this is the place?" Connor asked as he parked the jeep outside a dilapidated motel.

The welcome sign flickered on and off, on and off, sparking with each flash. Connor pressed his nose against the car window, peering out into the dark. "Demons normally go for somewhere with more, you know, class."

Niv's hands danced as he signed something. JD caught snatches of it – something about a camera maybe? He looked to Zek, who translated.

"He says it's definitely the place. He hacked the CCTV."

The boys had come to this run-down part of Chicago after DAD had been triggered by key phrases broadcast over the local police radio. People going missing. Increase in violent crime. Reports of people with black eyes. Check. Check. Check.

DAD, short for Demonic Activity Detector, was a highly

sophisticated computer program originally built by some of the finest minds at the National Security Agency to monitor terrorist activity. It had been adapted and renamed by Niv to meet the boys' unique interests. Bots scoured newsfeeds, forums, social networks and even some firewalled intranets that weren't supposed to be accessed by the public. If anyone posted anything relating to demons, Niv would be notified within a matter of minutes.

Niv held up his phone. The screen showed grainy black-and-white footage from a security camera covering the motel. Niv wound the footage back to fifteen minutes ago. The boys watched as a battered Ford pulled up and three white men dressed in black and a Latino woman wearing a long red skirt stepped out. They looked human, but that meant nothing. Most of the things the boys faced looked human. It wasn't until you looked into their eyes that you saw what they really were. The boys watched and waited till one of the figures turned their face to the camera. Completely black eyes stared back at them.

"Demons," Tom said with clear disgust in his voice. Tom was the most forgiving of them all, always looking for the good in everyone he met. But when it came to demons, his heart was ice-cold.

Niv pointed to his eyes and then the phone. *Keep watching.* A moment later, the demons dragged a teenage girl from the back seat of the Ford. JD flinched at seeing her fear, wanting to somehow jump into the screen and save her. She was dragged, kicking and screaming, across the parking lot and into room eight. The motel employed remote security guards who would only turn up if an alarm was triggered and the manager was nowhere to be seen. If any of the other guests had heard the girl's cries for help, they'd chosen to ignore them.

Fifteen minutes ago. They might already be too late.

"All right. Let's move."

The boys leaped out of the jeep, adjusting the neoprene half-masks and goggles they always wore on duty. Each boy had customized their own mask: JD's was simple urban camo, Tom's had a stylized Union Jack flag, Zek's looked like a grinning skull, Niv's had red flames creeping up the edges, while Connor's was white with a large brown moustache and he always topped it with his tatty red snapback.

They raced to the rear of the jeep and Niv threw open the tailgate. He hit a button and a hidden box slid out from under the back seat. An array of silver weapons glinted in the street lights. When going up against a demon guns didn't work – you needed salt or cold hard metal to send their souls screaming back to the Netherworld. Iron worked just as well, but silver had more style.

Zek and Niv handed them out. The three-pointed sais blades for Connor. A compound bow and quiver of black-tipped arrows for Tom. And JD's sword. He slid the katana out of its saya and felt the cool grip of the stingray skin that covered its handle under his fingers. That left the pair of engraved scimitars for the twins.

The curtains of the motel room were drawn and shadows moved inside.

Connor spun his twin sais, grinning wildly at the *whoosh* as they sliced the air. Niv hit a button on his phone and the blinking light on the security camera went dark. Now, the only person watching would be Gail. She'd be back at base, watching the feed from each of the boys' headcams.

When they first started hunting demons, Gail came with them, using every mission as a chance to train them. Now she came less and less, trusting them to take care of themselves and because, JD knew, she was training him up to take the lead. He didn't always like calling the shots, but he was good at it.

Slay pelted across the empty parking lot towards room eight, cracked tarmac crunching under foot. Using hand signals to communicate, JD pointed to the twins and directed them round the back. He, Connor and Tom would take the front.

JD crept up the steps to the door, Tom behind him and Connor bringing up the rear. He pressed his back against the wall between the door and the small window. It was half open and tatty orange curtains blew in the slight breeze. The sound of voices drifted out through the window and

JD leaned closer. It sounded like low, rhythmic chanting. A ritual. They'd have to move fast.

JD held out a fist with his thumb pointing out. The sign for a flash grenade. They'd blind the demons and pick them off while they were still blinking. Connor pulled the grenade from his belt and threw it through the window. They waited. A deafening explosion smashed all the windows out and filled the motel room with thick, orange smoke.

"I gave the sign for a flash grenade, Con," JD shouted over the ringing noise. "Not smoke, you idiot." The smoke in question was sodium chloride – salt – which demons hated. But it was hardly subtle.

"Oops." Connor grinned – he liked anything that made loud bangs, from his drum kit to his weapons – and jumped through the window.

Here's to you

"I'm serious, Naledi," Milly said. "It's total *Body Snatchers* here."

As soon as Milly had reached the safety of her room, she'd video-called her best friend back in London and told her all about her mother's weirdness.

"Aliens, huh?" Naledi mumbled through a yawn. It was the middle of the night in London. Naledi tolerated Milly's inability to remember the difference in time zones, but only when it was an emergency. "Do you think they'd take my mum too?"

"Come on, Nal, something is really weird with her. If it's not aliens then..." Milly stopped, replaying what she thought she'd seen downstairs.

"What?"

"Then maybe she's on drugs?"

Naledi said nothing for a moment, seeming to consider

the seriousness of what her friend had just said, then burst out laughing.

"I'm serious, Nal, she was being all huggy and…nice."

"Aren't you always saying you wish she was more like a proper mum?"

"Yes, but why now?"

"Chill, Mills," Naledi said, her image jittering as the connection broke up for a moment. "Your mum does this. Remember the time she got into minimalism and threw all your stuff out? Or when she got into crystals and covered the place in rocks. Being huggy is probably just her new phase."

"I wish she didn't have to drag me along for the ride, is all."

Naledi sighed. "I'd swap my mum for yours any day. Mine won't let me go anywhere without making me check in every five minutes. She lectured me for two hours this week about boys. At least yours lets you have a life."

"But only the life she wants for me. No pop music, no movies. And it's this Mourdant guy. I don't trust him. He wears sunglasses, Nal, indoors. Like, all the time. I'm starting to wonder if he's even got eyes behind them."

Naledi shook her head, her box braids dancing. "Mills, you know I love you and your off-the-chain imagination, but you're mental. And it's…" she checked her watched, "really stupid early here, so I'm going to crawl back into bed and you are going to find your chill."

A loud bang sounded downstairs, followed by the sound of Milly's mum's high-pitched laugh.

"Milly," her mother called, "come celebrate with us."

"Oh god, she's going to force me to drink champagne. Save me, Nal."

"You're perfectly capable of saving yourself, Mills. And I hardly think getting to drink champagne can be considered child abuse."

"I think I'll just hide in my room."

"Also a good plan. Catch you soon, Mills. Call me if she sprouts tentacles."

Milly said her goodbyes and hung up.

She missed her life in London. Missed the apartment in Notting Hill. But most of all, she missed Naledi. They'd only known each other for a year, but Naledi was the only person who'd ever got her. They'd originally bonded because they were both new at the school, but then discovered they both shared a secret passion for fantasy novels and conspiracy theories.

It wasn't even worth making friends here in Chicago to fill the Naledi-shaped hole in her life, as they would only be moving again as soon as her mother had another "clash of personalities".

The map pinned to her wall was covered in small red and blue pushpins marking all the places her mother had dragged her to. She'd moved ten times in the last five years. And in each new place, Milly was expected to fit in and find new friends. It was harder than ever this time. Three weeks since starting school and still the only people who knew her name were the teachers.

She didn't belong here. The truth was, Milly didn't belong anywhere. Her mother was French, her dad British-Chinese, and she had never stayed anywhere long enough to be able to call it home. She looked at all those little pins in the map, each marking a major city. But Milly wanted to travel for real. She wanted to go to Mongolia and see the eagle hunters. To Mexico and climb ancient temples. She wanted to see the world and have great adventures, not just follow in her mother's wake.

With a sigh, Milly changed out of her uniform and into her comfiest clothes: baggy tracksuit trousers and an old purple hoodie that had belonged to her dad. It was 9.30 p.m. on a Friday night and most other girls her age were probably out having fun, while she would be at home, doing her homework. Yet again. Not that she really minded, but it would be nice to have options.

"Milly!" her mother called again, more insistent this time.

"I'm doing homework," Milly shouted.

"*Stop being rude, we have guests,*" her mother shouted back in French.

Milly let out a grunt of frustration and stomped towards

her bedroom door. She threw it open and continued to stomp all the way down the stairs, making no attempt to hide how annoyed she was.

"There you are!" her mum said as she trudged into the living room. Mourdant lounged in a red-leather armchair, swinging a bottle of champagne back and forth. His head turned in her direction and she could feel his eyes behind the sunglasses boring into her skin. Alice was perched in the corner, staring into an empty glass as if she was wishing she could vanish into it. She swayed a little, her eyelids drooping like she was struggling to stay awake. Milly wondered how many glasses she'd drunk already.

"Oh, but, child, do you have to wear that hideous jumper?"

"I'm sorry, I'll just go and slip into one of my ballgowns, shall I?"

"So sarcastic, Milly. I don't know where you get that from."

"Me neither," Milly muttered.

Fact was she got it from her father. She and her dad used to have a lot of fun being sarcastic in sign language, drawing out the signs and exaggerating their facial expressions, while her mother had never picked up on it.

"Well, come, we promised you champagne." She pushed an empty glass into Milly's hand and waved her towards Mourdant.

The man unfolded himself from the chair and held out

the black bottle. Milly didn't want to accept anything from him – something about him made her skin crawl. But the sooner she got this over with, the sooner she could go back to her room.

She closed the distance between them and held out the glass. Mourdant poured, watching her all the while. Milly stared at her own reflection in his glasses; she looked so tiny, so afraid. Mourdant smiled, as if sensing her discomfort. The golden liquid filled half of the glass.

"Stop," Milly said.

Mourdant ignored her and continued to pour and pour.

"Stop," she said again.

Champagne filled the glass to the brim and then splashed over Milly's hand and onto the carpet. Only then did he stop pouring.

"To your mother," he said, raising the bottle in a toast.

Alice raised her empty glass and mumbled, "To mother."

Milly raised her own glass and brought it to her lips, pretending to take a sip.

"Drink up, Milly," Mourdant said, grabbing the base of her glass and tipping it so quickly that a mouthful of the fizzing liquid rushed into her mouth. She swallowed reflexively, and then coughed as the bubbles tickled her nose.

"Gentle, Mourdant," Milly's mother said. "This is her first taste of alcohol."

That wasn't true. She and Naledi had shared a can of

warm cider once. Neither of them had liked it much. Champagne, as far as she could tell, wasn't much better.

"Finish the whole glass, Milly," Mourdant said. "You wouldn't want such expensive champagne to go to waste."

Fear crept up Milly's spine. Why was he being so insistent about this? She looked to her mother for help, but she had started to hum and sway around the room. Alice was half asleep, her head lolling on her chest. Mourdant continued to stare at Milly.

She raised the glass to her lips again slowly, her hand shaking. She didn't know why, but she was certain that something very bad would happen if she drank the champagne. With his gaze boring into her, she tipped the glass, feeling the cold liquid fill her mouth. If she didn't think of something soon, she'd have no choice but to swallow.

A loud thud sounded as Alice fell off her chair. Mourdant turned around to look and Milly used that moment of distraction to spit out the champagne and tip the rest of the glass into a nearby vase.

She returned the glass to her lips and when Mourdant spun back around, she mimed swallowing.

"Hmm, lovely," she said, wiping her mouth with the back of her hand. "Although I don't think it's agreed with Alice."

Her mother glanced over at her PA. "Oh, yes, she's had a little too much."

Milly edged towards the door. "Can I go now?"

"Of course, *ma chérie*." Her mother kissed her on the top of her head. "Sleep well."

"Yes," Mourdant said, flashing one of his shark smiles, "sleep very well."

He looked at her over the rim of his glasses and she saw his eyes for the first time. She could have sworn they were completely jet-black.

Hit me with all you got

There was only one thing that came close to the high of performing onstage and that was dusting demons. Luckily for JD, he got to do both.

The demon's screech never left its mouth as its air supply was cut off along with its head. JD continued the arc of the sword strike, letting the momentum spin him around to bring the tip of the blade to the face of a second creature. Even through the yellow smoke, JD could see that this one was young in human terms, with skin still covered in acne. Eyes still watering from the salt grenade, the demon couldn't see JD in front of him. It bared stained, rotting teeth and charged – straight onto JD's blade. With a pathetic squeal, it slumped to the floor. Another demon frantically clawed the wall, as if trying to somehow scratch its way through. It never got a chance to find out if it could. A flash of Connor's sais and it toppled sideways. Which left one more. Tom took aim with his bow. A single arrow through a black eye and it was over.

The bodies of three men and one woman lay slumped on the floor. The smell of sulphur filled the room. That had taken less than thirty seconds. Now that the smoke had cleared, JD lifted his goggles to get a better view, but kept his mask in place.

"Not fair," Zek said, arriving through the bathroom door and surveying the scene. "Did you not think to leave any for us?"

"You can kill my one again if ya like," Connor said, pointing over his shoulder to the body oozing black blood. "You know, just to be sure."

"Given how sloppy you are, I might have to."

Niv appeared next to his brother and raised four fingers.

"Yep, only four," Tom said, answering Niv's question.

The bodies on the floor looked human, but JD knew that they'd been walking corpses from the moment the demons had possessed them. The cheap motel carpet had been ripped up and symbols marked on the floorboards in white chalk and blood. In the centre was a large pentagram scrawled with demonic writing. Looked like they'd arrived just in time to stop the ritual.

Demons were big into their rituals. Always summoning and sacrificing. Demons weren't able to enter the human world on their own – they had to be summoned. They also couldn't take possession of a human uninvited. They had to be let in, sometimes willingly, other times less so. As soon as a demon crossed over, it would go around recruiting, manipulating or tricking humans into giving up their souls to become hosts for more demons from the Netherworld.

Low-ranking demons could cross over into this world with no more than a few simple words from a human dumb enough to recite them. Say the right words and make the right marks and you'd be a demon hand-puppet in no time. Demons even left summoning rituals on the internet for anyone to find. And lots of people did. Since Slay had been in the States, they'd had to save a number of drunken frat boys who thought summoning a demon would make for a fun time.

But summoning something stronger, like a demon prince, that took serious power. According to Gail, the last time a demon prince had been summoned was back in the 1930s and that had nearly ended the world. No one had seen anything so powerful since. But the creatures were there, in the Netherworld, just waiting.

A choked sobbing drew JD's attention to the corner of the room. The girl was still alive, huddled in a corner, shaking. She was fourteen, maybe fifteen. Make-up ran down her face in dark tracks. In all the excitement, JD had forgotten about her.

Tom hadn't. Tom never did.

"Hey," Tom said, kneeling down next to the girl. She screamed and tried to scrabble away, terrified. "It's okay. You're safe now. I've got you." He lifted his goggles so the girl could see his eyes weren't black. "What's your name?"

The girl stared at Tom. "I'm Hope," she said, her voice shaking. "My arm hurts."

Blood trickled out of a semicircular cut on her arm. It looked as if the demons had tried to force her into becoming a host, but they'd not been able to complete the mark. Tom cleaned the wound before pulling a bandage out of the kit on his belt and wrapping it around her arm.

"Well, Hope, listen to me." A melodic quality came over Tom's voice. "You're fast, fast asleep at home and you just had a horrible dream."

"A dream," the girl said, her voice soft and sleepy.

"You've been sleepwalking, Hope, and we need to get you back into bed." He helped her to her feet and started leading her out of the room.

"You have beautiful eyes," the girl said, gazing up at him.

"That's nice." He looked back at the boys. "I'll put her in a cab."

JD smirked. Tom wasn't the hottest of the bunch, he wasn't the funniest, but he did have a way with girls. Not that he was even remotely aware of it, which JD thought was for the best. He also had a way with hypnotism. Gail had tried to teach the other boys how to do it, but only Tom had

41

the knack – something to do with those bright green eyes and the gentle tone of his voice. JD didn't have the patience for it. He stuck to hitting things and left the talking to the others.

"Have we been here before?" Zek said, turning back to the room. "I recognize the delightful decor."

JD followed the direction of his gaze to the grimy, striped wallpaper. Before the band had really taken off, they'd stayed in places like this.

"Maybe," JD said. "If so, I've tried to wipe it from my memory."

"Oh, I don't know," Zek said, patting the wall. "It has a certain Stephen King charm."

Niv's hands flashed, finishing by drawing a finger across his neck and miming blood splashing over the walls. JD didn't know much sign language, but he often got the gist when Niv was telling a particularly twisted joke.

"Eww," Zek said, wiping his hand up and down Niv's back.

"Okay, enough messing," JD said, as Niv tried to push Zek's face into the wall. "Clean-up procedure. Connor—"

Connor groaned. "Why is it always me?"

At fifteen, Connor was the youngest of the group, even though he didn't look it. He was the tallest and broadest of the boys, having had a freakish growth spurt a few months after joining them. JD remembered Connor as he'd been back when they first met: a bony little thing with huge blue eyes staring out from a round, dirty face. Now he was all muscles.

"I was going to say, 'Connor, go get the jeep while the twins and I bag and fry'. But if you want to do the duty?"

"No, no!" Connor said, holding his hand up. "Getting the jeep is grand." He rushed out before JD had a chance to change his mind. It was *technically* legal to have a learner's permit at fifteen in Illinois and Connor, who had learned to drive the family tractor when he was twelve, was making the most of it.

A moment later tail lights shone through the small front window, lighting up the grubby room as Connor backed the jeep up. He killed the engine and the room was thrown into darkness once more.

JD and Niv opened the back of the jeep and dragged out three disposal sacks. They were like body bags, only made from PBI – the stuff they made astronauts' suits out of – and designed to withstand intense heat. Roll a body in there, throw in a mini incendiary grenade and zip it up, then it was only a matter of disposing of the ashes. No bodies to be found and the demons' victims would just be added to the endless list of the missing.

JD often wondered why they didn't go public about the existence of demons – at least it would give the families of those possessed or killed some kind of closure. But Gail insisted they keep it quiet. She'd explained it to him four years ago, in the police station in Manchester – where he was being held after his aunt and her boyfriend had been killed by demons.

"If the public found out that these creatures walk among us there would be panic. Before we knew it, they'd be burning their neighbours and shooting their bosses just to be sure. Have you ever read about the witch-hunts of the Dark Ages? It would be like that. Only with YouTube."

So JD and the others went around taking down demon after demon and clearing up the mess so that no one would find out. All part of the job.

"She'll be okay. I hypnotized her – she'll only snap back out of it when she's home in bed with no memory of tonight," Tom said, coming back into the room. "My Derren Brown stuff is coming on a treat." He waggled his fingers.

JD kneeled down next to one of the bodies and pushed up its sleeve.

"We've got a mark," he said. Sure enough, there was a tattoo: a looping circle with overlapping ends. Each of the other bodies would have sigils like this one – marks that allowed the demons to take possession of their bodies. Some were unwilling sacrifices, like the girl had clearly been. Most were idiots who branded themselves, becoming willing hosts. What they didn't realize till it was too late was that as soon as a demon stepped in, the human soul was kicked out and lost for ever.

The boys bore marks of their own – but instead of inviting demons in, their tattoos kept demons out.

"Same mark on this one," Tom said, pointing at another body. "I don't recognize it."

Niv took a picture of the symbol with his phone and JD watched as he ran it through DAD. After a few moments the phone screen flashed.

NOT RECOGNIZED

"Maybe Gail will know what it is?" JD said.

Zek rubbed at the tattoo. Black pigment flecked away. "The ink is fresh."

"Stupid," JD said quietly, shaking his head. The man had probably summoned the demon thinking it would bring him fame or fortune. All it had brought him was death. When would people learn? There was no doing a deal with demons – the demons always won.

"Check this out," Zek said, holding up an open wallet. "He's got a Lyric Opera pass. ID says he's security."

Niv picked a baseball cap up off the floor. It had the word *Lyric* stitched on the front in gold thread.

"Opera lovers, it seems," Tom said.

"Didn't I tell ya demons had class?" Connor said, from inside of the jeep.

"Hmm," JD said. They'd have to look into what was going

on at the opera house. "Okay, let's fry these guys and get back to Agatha." JD rolled the first body into a bag, pulled the pin on a grenade and threw it in, then zipped the bag up quickly, trying not to look too hard at the dead guy's face. A face that in the next few days would be appearing on missing posters and in JD's nightmares.

With a dull *thuff* the bag expanded, then slowly deflated, a small curl of foul-smelling smoke drifting through the zip.

Hold on tight

Milly closed her bedroom door behind her and leaned against it. Then, as an afterthought, she locked it. Her hands still shook and she felt a troubling fogginess tugging at her mind. She hadn't realized champagne could be so strong.

She took a few deep breaths and tried to calm down. She was overreacting. She was always overreacting. Sure, Mourdant was creepy and that whole business with the champagne had been so weird, but it was over now and she was safely in her own room. He'd be gone soon and tomorrow she would talk to her mum and insist that that man never stepped foot in this house again. Okay, so she already knew how *that* would go: her mother would tell her to stop being so dramatic and ignore her. Like always. But she would at least try.

She stepped away from the door and shook her hands and head, trying to brush off the feeling that Mourdant was still watching her. The sharp tang of champagne lingered, more bitter than she had expected. Why had Mourdant been so adamant that she drink it? What did she really know about him anyway? He'd appeared from nowhere, persuading her mother to fire her old manager, and then suddenly they were here in Chicago and she was signing some new, exciting contract. Was he even a real manager? Well, there was one way to find out.

Milly walked over to her desk, stumbling against her bed a little, and sat down. She fired up her laptop and typed one word into the search bar.

Mourdant.

The first two pages were filled with results about a nineteenth-century Scottish lord, the third and fourth pages were no help either. Milly refined the search by adding the word *Manager*. This time, all she got was information on an accounting firm in New York. She scrolled and scrolled until her eyes started to blur. If only she knew his first name.

"I mean, come on," she said out loud, "who doesn't have a first name?"

There was nothing on this guy. Not so much as a tweet. He didn't, according to the internet, exist. It all made a weird kind of sense. He had to be a conman, manipulating her mum into…what? Giving all her money to him? What was in that contract that he was so excited about? Milly knew she should storm down there, grab that thing from him and tear it to shreds. But what would be the point? Her mother would only shout at her and send her back to her room before signing a fresh copy. Besides, she was so tired.

Not for the first time, Milly felt the twisting stab of grief over losing her dad. If he were here, none of this would be happening. If he were here, she wouldn't be alone. Even if he couldn't have persuaded her mother to get rid of Mourdant, then at least Milly and her dad would have enjoyed themselves making fun of the man in sign language. Three years since he had died and she missed him so much that it often felt like there was a great gaping hole in her chest where her heart should have been.

She focused back on the internet results. Weariness tugged at her mind and she rubbed at her itching eyes. She wasn't going to give up. She paused for a moment before adding another phrase into the search. *Black eyes.*

She scanned the results and felt a cold dread settle in her stomach. Nothing directly related to Mourdant, but pages and pages of reports about people with black eyes. Words jumped out at her. *Ghosts. Demons. Evil.* She pushed her laptop away. This was getting out of hand. She was getting carried away, as usual.

Her head pounded and she struggled to keep her eyes open. All she wanted to do was sleep. This could wait till tomorrow. She would find out who Mourdant was and what he was up to tomorrow. She had to sleep now. She dragged herself over to her bed; her limbs felt heavy and awkward. She would just sleep in these clothes. What did it matter anyway? The light was still on but she didn't have the energy to get up and turn it off. Instead, she pulled a pillow over her head to block it out.

She felt like she was floating there in the darkness. This was nothing like the feeling when she and Nal had drunk that cider. This was more like when she'd been in hospital to have her tonsils out. More like she was…

The thought was interrupted by the chime of a new email from her phone. Pushing the pillow aside, she stretched her hand as far as she could, her fingertips just brushing the edge of the phone. She dragged it closer and, finally, pulled it onto the bed with her. It took a while for her to be able to focus on the words. They floated and drifted like she was looking at them underwater.

To: Lyudmila Durand-Lin
From: <Undisclosed>
Subject: You're not safe

Milly hesitated. It was probably just a spam email. But… maybe?

Dear Lyudmila Durand-Lin,
We have intercepted your recent online communications

and it appears you may be in danger. We have also detected unusual activity in your local area. If you concur with this analysis you should reply to this email immediately and people who can help will be in touch. In the meantime, we also recommend you remove yourself from your current situation. If this is not possible, find a safe place and lock your doors.

We hope this email has not reached you too late.

This is an automated message.

Thank you for your attention.

DAD.

Milly blinked, trying to focus her blurry eyes, and read it again. She forced a bitter laugh and closed the email. Not only did she have a creepy conman in her house, now someone else was having her on? Bit of a sick joke, really. Why would anyone want to freak a stranger out like that? And what did this DAD, whoever he was, mean about intercepting "online communications"? She hoped it wasn't some stalker like they'd been warned about in general studies.

"Delete," she said out loud, hitting the little dustbin symbol, consigning the message to the trash.

She placed her phone on the table and lay back on the bed. Tonight sucked. She felt clammy and her stomach gurgled uncomfortably. Her body was begging for sleep, but her mind resisted, pushing against the weariness. That message kept niggling at her. She opened her email again and went to the trash folder. Sandwiched between spam about prescription drugs and a fresh request from a Nigerian prince was DAD's mail. She read it for a third time.

In danger.
People who can help.
Lock your doors.

She struggled to sit up, rubbing at her eyes, fighting against the tug of sleep. Maybe she should take this seriously? Report it to someone or at least tell her mum?

She heard singing from downstairs, her mother's voice at full volume. If anything could keep her awake it was this. Her mother never cared if her singing bothered Milly, it always came first. Milly didn't recognize the part her mother was singing. It sounded more like chanting than an aria. It was unlike anything she'd heard in her life. Hypnotic, uncomfortable. The notes made her skin itch. She wanted to block it out and yet couldn't stop listening to it. It cut through her weariness like a knife.

She crawled off the bed and headed for the door. Her mother, accompanied by the piano now, ramped up, hitting her world-famous high F.

And that's when the screaming started.

Whenever I close my eyes

The boys called their tour bus Agatha and it was the closest thing JD and the others had to a home. It was currently parked under a heavily-graffitied railway bridge on the east side of Chicago. Inside, hidden from the world, the boys and Gail went over the mission.

"They were from the opera house?" Gail said.

"At least two of them," JD said.

"Interesting."

"What's interesting?" Connor asked.

"Your face," Zek said, then quickly dodged Connor's fist. "No, I mean it. Look at all those freckles. In my country, we would have thought you a freak of nature. Maybe even burned you as a witch."

"No one in Morocco burns people as witches," Tom said. "Stop winding him up. What were you saying, Gail?"

"We'll have to go and pay the Lyric a visit tomorrow.

Maybe they would be interested in a gig from Slay?"

"We've never played an opera house," Zek said. "Fancy."

"Don't get distracted by the cover story," Gail said. "There's definitely something weird going on."

"We love weird," Tom said, plucking a series of eerie notes on his guitar. Tom was the real musical talent in the group. He could play almost every instrument ever made, while the only thing JD could get a decent noise out of was his beloved Gibson Hummingbird.

The vibrations of the Loop train running overhead shook the bus.

"All right," Gail said, tapping her rings against the silver wolf-head of her cane. "Let's play this one by the book till we know what we're dealing with. I want you all to be especially cautious." She gave Connor an extra stern stare.

"What?" the Irish boy said, clutching his hands to his chest. "I did nothing!"

"No, but I saw your face when we passed that bike park on the way into town," their manager said. "No wandering off till we work out what's happening, okay? I want you all where I can keep my eye on you." She tapped next to her one good eye.

"All right, all right," he said. "I'll stay here, like a good boy."

Gail leaned forward and kissed his forehead. "You can throw yourself off something really tall in the next state we go to, I promise."

Connor's face lit up. "I've been dying to try out my new wingsuit."

JD shook his head. Connor had a weird kind of death wish. He was always throwing himself down things and off things. He said it was his way of dealing with their wild lives, but JD sometimes wondered if there wasn't more to it than that.

"Okay, we'll keep scanning for any more activity and head to the opera house in the morning. But now, get some rest. I want you on sparkling form for your interview with John tomorrow." Gail stood, flexing her injured leg.

"I'm always on sparkling form," Tom mumbled. "It's JD who never says more than three words."

"Maybe with a good sleep he'll be moved to say four words," Gail said, winking at JD. "Goodnight, boys."

Zek was already out cold in his bunk. That boy could sleep anywhere. He'd once fallen asleep in a tree when he was supposed to be looking out for a demon. It had turned out to be just an old woman who'd wandered off from a care home, but the boys had given him grief about it for weeks after anyway.

Connor leaped up onto the bunk above JD, causing the springs to complain wildly. He did this every night, but JD still expected the bunk to come crashing down on him one day.

"May angels watch me through the night," Connor said, just as he always did.

"And wake me with the morning light," Tom and JD replied together.

The prayer was how Connor's mother had always tucked him into bed. Now it was how all the boys said goodnight. JD wondered if he would be able to sleep without the comfort of the ritual.

He hadn't been sleeping much lately anyway. He kept having nightmares about the little boy in Nebraska. They'd been too late to stop the boy being possessed and the failure had eaten away at JD every night since. He still saw the boy's young face twisted by the evil that had taken over it, black bulging eyes and ragged lips chewed purple. Even though they'd killed the demon and stopped it ruining any more lives, it wasn't enough. Their job was supposed to be about saving people, but lately it felt like the demons were winning. Every time they took out one, two more seemed to pop up in their place. Zek called it demonic *whack-a-mole* and he wasn't far off. One day, JD planned to find a way into the demonic Netherworld and take the fight to them.

In the bunk opposite, Tom put his guitar aside and paused before lying down. "Don't, Jay," he said softly.

"Don't what?" JD whispered back.

"Keep blaming yourself. I know that look. The boy was dead before we got there." Sometimes JD wondered if Tom could read his mind. "Just get some shut-eye. You won't be America's hottest teenager for long without your beauty sleep." Tom threw him a big grin.

The boys had been teasing JD for weeks after a magazine named him top of their *Hot Teens* list.

"That's the *world's* hottest teenager, thank you very much," JD said, slipping his hands behind his head.

"How could I forget?" Tom mumbled, and then rolled over.

Niv was the only one still up, scribbling away, a small light throwing his sharp features into relief. Niv pretended he was ice-cold, always the first to roll his dark eyes when anyone got overemotional. But the poems he wrote in that old leather notebook said different. *You've gathered up the pieces of my broken heart and made me whole*, was the chorus to "Heart Strike", a song that had been number one in twelve different countries. JD wondered how all those kids who danced to it at proms would feel if they knew it was really about the time Slay had gone up against a golem.

Niv pointed at the light.

"No, keep it on," JD said. "I don't mind."

As desperate as his body was for sleep, he didn't want to close his eyes just yet. He knew that all the faces of the people he'd failed to save would be waiting for him in the dark.

JD pushed the images out of his mind and rolled over, pulling the pillow with him. Another L train rattled overhead, shaking the bus. He found the sound strangely soothing.

He was just drifting off when he heard a high-pitched

ringing. He tried to block it out. But he couldn't ignore the insistent shaking of his arm. "All right, already," he said, twisting around to face Niv. The guitarist was pointing to his phone where an alert from DAD was flashing.

POSSIBLE DEMONIC ATTACK.
RESPOND IMMEDIATELY.

JD grabbed the phone and scanned the report.

"No beauty sleep tonight, boys," he shouted, waking everyone up. "We have some more demons to send back to hell."

You're in my blood

Milly froze at her bedroom door. The screams didn't sound like her mother – maybe it was Alice who was hurt. She had to go down and help. The screaming was getting louder, more desperate. And yet Milly couldn't make herself turn the handle. She was scared. More scared than she had ever been in her life. She felt instinctively that whatever was happening downstairs was beyond bad.

And then the screaming stopped.

In the silence, Milly felt the fear loosen its grip. It was okay. Alice was okay. There was nothing to worry about. Nothing at all. She looked down at her phone, still in her hand, and remembered the email.

Lock your doors.

She was just freaking herself out now. The email combined with her stupid imagination was causing her to think of all sorts of strange things. Impossible things.

She gave herself a mental shake and yanked the door open before she had a chance to change her mind.

From downstairs, she heard a man's voice – Mourdant's. She couldn't make out what he was saying, but his tone was sharp and urgent.

She crept along the landing and towards the stairs so she could hear more clearly. She hadn't been in the house long enough to work out which parts of the floor creaked, so she lowered each foot into place carefully, hoping not to make a sound.

When she got to the banisters, she bent down and peered through the bars into the hallway. What she saw didn't make any sense at first.

Mourdant had one hand wrapped around Alice's neck and another across her mouth. The young woman struggled and writhed in his grip, but he was too strong for her. Milly's mother stood in front of them, shaking her head.

"I can't. I can't," Milly heard her say.

"Do it, Isobel. Do it and you will have everything I have promised you. Fame, fortune, youth. Everything. It will be worth it."

"You said she would be asleep. You said the champagne would knock her out. I can't, not with her looking at me. No, I don't know what I was thinking, I can't do this." It was then that Milly saw something glinting in her mother's hand. A knife.

"We made a deal," Mourdant snarled.

"I'm sorry, but I'm not a murderer."

Mourdant let out a loud sigh. "Do I have to do everything? Very well."

Keeping his grip on Alice's throat with one hand, he grabbed Milly's mother's wrist with the other. As soon as Alice's mouth was free, she started screaming again, screeching for someone, anyone to help. And now Milly's mother was screaming too.

"No!" She sobbed, as Mourdant dragged her closer, closer. "I won't, I can't!" Mourdant shifted his grip on her wrist, the knife still glinting in her hand.

"Please, no. Take anything you want, money, anything, please don't make me do this!"

"You do not break a deal with The Mourdant." And with that, the man plunged the knife Isobel was holding into Alice's chest.

Milly looked away before the deed was done. She heard a sound like the slicing of a watermelon. And then, stillness.

When she dared to look back, Alice lay on the floor in a pool of blood, a black hole in her chest. Milly covered her mouth to try to stop the scream of terror escaping. It couldn't be. Mourdant was holding a human heart! She must have been imagining it. But then she heard Mourdant speak.

"And now make the mark as I told you. DO IT!"

As if Mourdant's hands were still forcing her, Milly's

mother turned the blood-covered knife on herself, carving into her arm. When she was finished, she dropped the blade to the floor.

"There, there it's done, God forgive me, it's done. Now what?"

"Now," Mourdant said, a cruel smile twisting his lips, "we say goodbye."

"Goodbye? But I—" Milly's mother's words were cut off as she threw her head back and let out a terrible screech. What looked like black smoke drifted up from between the old floorboards and curled around her, up her legs and wrapped around her arm. The smoke formed tendrils that caressed the bloody symbol she'd cut into her arm and pushed its way under her skin. Black veins branched out from the mark, down her arm to her hand and all the way up till the veins on her neck turned black too. Then, with a rush, the rest of the smoke poured into her mouth, into her eyes and nostrils, till every last black thread disappeared inside her.

When the last curl of darkness was gone, Milly's mother closed her mouth and straightened up.

A change came over her body. She looked taller somehow, more regal. She rolled her shoulders back, stretched her neck and arms as if waking after a long sleep. She moved with a snakelike grace Milly had never seen in her mother before. She opened her eyes and they shone black-silver, like haematite.

"Welcome back," Mourdant said, falling to one knee and bowing his head, "Zyanya, Priestess of Tezcatlipoca." The name dripped off Mourdant's tongue like flesh off a rotting corpse, chilling Milly's blood.

"How long have I been in darkness?"

Milly didn't recognize the voice coming from her mother's lips. Gone was the thick French accent. Instead, her words sounded sweet, like honey.

Milly didn't know what on earth was going on. But she knew one thing. That woman was not her mother.

"Centuries, my priestess. But I have brought you back. I found you a willing host, strong enough to contain your spirit so that you may finally complete the ritual."

The woman, who could no longer be Milly's mother, looked down at her hands, then ran them across her face and down her body. "Strong, yes." Then she looked down at Mourdant and lay her hand on his head, as if bestowing a blessing upon him. "You have done well. My lord Tezcatlipoca shall reward you." Milly shuddered at the use of that name again. "Rise, for we have work to do."

Mourdant got to his feet. "I have already tracked down the blade. Once it is returned to you, nothing can stand in your way."

The woman took a deep breath, and sighed. "At last, I shall finish that which was denied me."

Milly couldn't process what she was hearing. She fought

63

against the fear freezing her in place and backed away – only to trip over a rug.

"Who is there?"

She scrabbled to her feet and ran, faster than she had ever run before, heading for her bedroom. She slammed the door and twisted the lock. She remembered the estate agent making a big fuss over the door handles being salvaged from eighteenth-century French houses – well, Milly didn't care where they had come from, only that the lock would hold. She looked around for something to block the door. She tried the wardrobe first – a huge, carved oak affair. It didn't budge. She had more luck with the bed. She shoved it in place, not caring that the cast-iron legs scratched deep grooves into the ash floorboards. One last crunching shove and it was in place.

She had to get help. She remembered she was still holding her phone and dialled 911 as fast as her shaking hands would allow.

It only rang twice before she was put through. "What is the nature of your emergency?"

"There are, are…people in my house and they have black eyes and…I don't know what they are. Aliens or something."

There was a pause on the other end of the line, followed by a sigh. "Prank-calling the emergency services is an offence, miss."

"I swear, they just ripped a woman's heart out. Please, you have to come."

"We have your location. We'll send a patrol car to check on the situation, but if this is some kind of game then you will be charged with wasting police time." The line went dead.

Milly looked down at the phone helplessly. She didn't think one patrol car would be enough. She remembered the email. She opened and reread the message. *People who can help.* What did she have to lose?

She was mid reply when her door handle rattled.

"Come out." That sickly-sweet voice that was nothing like her mother's.

"Um…no?"

"We have something wonderful to show you." Mourdant's voice crept through the gaps of the door as if trying to find a way in. "Something truly wonderful. Come on out." The door handle rattled again.

"No, no, really, I'd rather not."

"Then we", the woman's voice boomed, "will come in."

A slam made the door shake. The bed shifted an inch. Milly braced herself between the bed and the far wall, pushing the iron frame back against the door with her legs. She needed help. And fast.

She hit reply.

To: <Undisclosed>
From: Lyudmila Durand-Lin
Subject: Re: You're not safe

HELP ME. PLEASE! YOU WERE RIGHT!

She chewed on the skin around her thumbnail before refreshing her mail. There was no way this "DAD" could have received the email and replied in just three seconds, but Milly kept dragging the page down, refreshing it over and over. A third slam made her nearly drop her phone. The door wasn't going to hold much longer.

Finally, an email pinged back.

To: Lyudmila Durand-Lin
From: <Undisclosed>
Subject: Re: Re: You're not safe

THANK YOU FOR YOUR MESSAGE. HELP IS ON ITS WAY.

Who was on their way?

As if in answer to her question she heard a roaring noise – followed by what sounded like something smashing through the front of her house.

If I come a-knockin'

The house was silent. That was never a good sign. As long as people were screaming, they were still breathing. Which meant there was still something that could be done. JD hoped they weren't too late. Again.

The house was old, maybe even Victorian, which was unusual around here. It had once been impressive, but was now faded, with flaking paint and ivy clawing at the brickwork. Large glass double doors were the only improvement that had been made in years. Which at least meant getting in would be easy.

"Hit it," JD said to Connor.

"Aw, but she's new," Connor said, stroking the dashboard.

JD fixed Connor with one of his unimpressed looks.

"All right, all right." Connor slammed on the gas and the jeep hurtled towards the front of the house. A moment before the impact, Connor hit a button and two large spikes shot out from under the bumper. Glass rained down like diamonds as the jeep bounced over the threshold. It screeched to a halt on the marble floor of the entrance hall, the headlights illuminating two figures standing at the top of a grand, curved staircase – a male and a female.

The boys kicked open the doors of the jeep and leaped out, weapons ready.

"Go, Priestess," the male said. "I will handle this."

The female vaulted over the banisters, long dark hair trailing behind her, and landed gracefully before sprinting away. She moved unnaturally fast for someone of her build, racing across the hallway and towards the back of the house. The male – tall, lean and wearing dark glasses even though it was night – wasn't going anywhere. They'd have to deal with him first. He walked slowly down the stairs, adjusting his cuffs.

"I take it you are the same children who dispatched four of my disciples earlier tonight? You have caused me a mild inconvenience, I'll give you that."

"Children, are we?" Zek said, spinning his scimitar around in a circle. "Well these children are about to send your butt back to hell, just like we did your lackeys."

"Zek," JD said warningly. There was no point antagonizing demons. Besides, JD wanted to know how this one had seen through their disguise. Masked and tooled up, they certainly didn't look like children.

The male demon seemed unfazed. He stopped in the middle of the staircase and smiled a dazzling smile. "Wait, I have seen you boys before. Aren't you…?" He clapped his hands together. "It can't be! My, my, this is wonderful."

"What are you talking about?" Tom said. "We've never set eyes on you before."

"No, but I have been watching you for some time. Quite the meteoric rise. I can see now why your manager was so adamant in rejecting my offer. What a shame I shall have to kill you all tonight. You would have made truly extraordinary hosts."

JD looked to Tom and the other boys. How did this demon know who they were?

"Oh, you're wondering how I can see past those silly masks of yours? Boys, you don't think these eyes look at your pathetic human bodies, do you?" He pulled his sunglasses off and tucked them into his top pocket. Jet-black eyes twinkled back at them. "They look right into your souls." With that, he flicked two fingers in Tom's direction. His mask and goggles flew off, smashing against the wall. "There is no hiding from me."

Tom stepped back, stunned. They'd never come up against demons with so much power before. Still, as Gail said, the bigger they were, the harder they fell. Magic tricks or not, it was five against one and this demon was going down.

JD strode forward, his blade at the ready. "Niv, Zek, see if you can track the woman. Connor, find the girl. Tom, you're with me." He didn't need to check that the others would follow his orders; they always did.

As he reached the bottom of the stairs he picked up his pace, charging towards the demon. Just as he placed a foot on the first step, the creature jumped up and spun over their heads. JD twisted to watch him soar through the air and land on the floor behind them.

The demon straightened up and brushed an invisible fleck of dust off his silver suit.

JD grimaced and strode back towards the man. Tom hadn't moved; he just kept looking between the step where the man had been and where he was standing now.

"Cool," he said.

JD threw him a disapproving look as he passed.

"Well it was," Tom muttered under his breath, taking his place by JD's side. They weren't going to let this thing get away this time.

JD lunged, his sword an extension of his arm, but the demon dodged effortlessly. Tom drew back his bow and let an arrow go, but the demon batted it out of the air as if swatting an annoying fly. This was going to need a different approach. JD pulled a flash grenade off his belt. He glanced at Tom, remembering just in time that he wasn't wearing his goggles. Tom closed his eyes and turned away, just as JD let it fly.

"Dodge this!"

The room exploded in a bright white light. While JD's eyes were protected from the glare by his goggles, the demon wasn't so lucky. Those black eyes were sensitive to light. The creature hissed and turned away, giving JD the opening he needed to attack. He stepped in and swung his sword, aiming for the neck. At the last moment, the demon stepped away so JD's blade only made contact with an arm, slicing through the silver sleeve. JD saw a flash of black blood.

The demon tutted. "You have ruined my favourite suit."

JD was seriously starting to hate this guy.

He swung again, feinting low and then changing at the last moment to strike high. Tom fired one, two more arrows. Both missed. The demon was too fast, somersaulting again until he was standing in the smashed doorway.

"While I could do this all night," he said, "I'm afraid I have places to be, rituals to orchestrate. Perhaps my friends can keep you entertained." He raised two slim fingers to his lips and blew, letting out a high-pitched whistle.

Through the remains of the front door burst two huge men dressed in black bomber jackets, both with the same gold *Lyric* lettering they'd seen on the dead guy's baseball cap back in the motel. They snarled and blinked black eyes.

JD took the one on the right while Tom went left. The demons were big but slow – the kind the boys were used to fighting. JD sliced the first one in half, from shoulder to hip, with a graceful strike of his sword. The creature made a small surprised squeak before toppling to the floor. Tom didn't even bother drawing his bow. Instead, he struck out with an arrow in his hand, plunging it into the neck of the second demon. There was a spurt of black blood and the demon sank to the floor, clutching at its throat. JD finished it off without even looking.

Then he glanced back to the doorway – it was empty. He raced outside and looked down the driveway. Nothing. The silver-suited demon had got away.

"Dammit!" JD shouted, slamming the door frame with his fist.

"Um…"

He turned to see Zek standing by the bottom of the stairs.

"Did you get her?"

"Sorry, Jay, she was right in front of us and then…" He blew on his fingers as if blowing away smoke.

JD shook his head. This hunt had been a total failure. Unless… "Connor!" he shouted. "Connor, have you found her?" There was no reply from Connor. Tom called back instead from a room off the hall.

"JD, you need to see this."

JD followed Tom's voice into a large living room. Three of the walls were covered in large oil paintings while the fourth bore a huge TV screen.

Tom pointed at a body. This had to be the girl who had

called for their help. She lay face up, blood pooling all around her, a large hole in her chest. JD curled his hands into tight fists, wanting to strike out at something, anything. They'd failed her. They failed at everything.

Tom crouched down and laid a gentle hand on the girl's shoulder, moving her hair aside so he could see her face.

He gasped. "It's not her. The girl we came here for, Lyudmila, was it? Report said she was sixteen and mixed race." Niv had hacked the girl's Facebook on the way over and they had all read up on her. "This woman is white and early twenties."

"So," JD said, a flutter of hope swelling in his stomach. Maybe they weren't too late after all. "Where's our girl?"

(Up to bat) For your love

Milly's heart pounded so hard she didn't know how it was managing to stay in her chest. She'd heard crashing and shouting and thudding from downstairs. But now there was just silence. And in some ways that was even worse.

The minutes stretched out agonizingly as she waited, her back pressed up against the wall. After five minutes of hearing nothing, she risked moving. The freezing panic of fear was being slowly replaced with a determination to survive. That couldn't have been her mother she'd seen doing those terrible things – her mother was overbearing and impossible, but she wasn't a killer. Milly's mind went back to the dumb idea that her mother had been taken over by aliens. Maybe it wasn't such a dumb idea after all. If that thing downstairs wasn't her mother, it meant the real Isobel Durand was in terrible danger. And Milly had to help her. She couldn't hide in this room for the rest of her life. There

74

had to be something in here she could arm herself with. The time for hiding was over. She had to fight back.

She glanced around. The majority of the room was filled with books, but what use were they now? Even the heavier hardbacks wouldn't have much impact against knives. Her dad had called her his little bookworm and teased her about never seeing the sun. He had loved the outdoors and had always tried to get her to go out more...which reminded her. The baseball bat he had given her for her thirteenth birthday. The last birthday they'd had together.

She raced over to her wardrobe, slid open the door, and winced when a jumble of shoes and books fell down on her head. All stuff her mother had told her to throw away before the move but she'd kept hold of out of spite. Thinking of her mother felt like someone had reached into her stomach and twisted. What had Mourdant done to her? Whatever it was, he was going to pay. Milly wasn't scared any more. Now she was angry.

She pushed all the clutter aside and pulled out the bat. She twisted her hands around the grip, finding the perfect position like her dad had taught her. The tape was coming away in places. Filled with rage, she strode towards the door. She'd lost one parent and she wasn't about to lose another. If she had to beat whatever that thing was out of her mother, she'd do it.

With a kick less powerful than she had hoped, she shoved

the bed aside and dragged the door open.

The landing was empty, but she could hear voices coming from downstairs. Hefting the reassuring weight of the baseball bat in her hands, she headed towards the sound. The voices became clearer: the murmur of people chatting. Mourdant and the thing in her mother's body maybe? The anger bubbled hotter.

She lifted the bat over her shoulder and picked up her pace. Before she knew it, she was running down the stairs, roaring like a crazed person. Ready to hit and bash and crush and destroy anyone or anything she found there.

She charged into the living room, screaming, bat raised. Three figures stood with their backs to her. She swung the bat back and let it fly.

The head she was aiming for ducked at the last second and the bat went wide, smashing into a wooden dresser, shattering glass. She swung again, aiming for one of the other figures. He raised an arm to block her blow and, quicker than she'd ever seen anyone move, grabbed the bat and twisted it out of her grip.

"Whoa!" he said.

Before she could do anything else, arms grabbed her from behind. She kicked and thrashed, trying to shake them off.

"It's okay," the boy who had grabbed the bat said, "you're safe."

The haze of rage faded and through it Milly saw a slim white boy with curly blond hair and a wide smile and sparkling green eyes. She recognized him. She'd seen this face staring back at her from magazines, billboards and from her own TV just a few hours ago. But that couldn't be possible... Standing next to him was a tall, dark-skinned figure with swirls shaved into the side of his head. He wore a half-mask with a grinning skull across it and goggles, hiding his face. And yet...

The arms pinning her let go and a third boy stepped forward. He was a mirror image of the boy with the shaved head. They also had matching tattoos snaking up their arms, the black patterns blending seamlessly with the engravings on their curved swords. Twins.

Milly blinked to check she wasn't imagining things, but, yes, they were carrying swords. All three boys wore black combats and heavy black boots. None of this was making any kind of sense. Why were they here? *How* were they here?

"It's okay," the blond boy said, one hand raised, the other holding the bat down by his side. Milly made out a British accent. "It's all okay." He flipped the bat over in his hand and returned it to her, handle first.

Milly took it. "But you're...you're..." she stuttered.

"We're Slay," a voice said from behind her. "And we're here to help."

In it together

There was no point pretending. With his mask and goggles off, this girl had clearly recognized Tom.

JD pulled off his own mask and ran his fingers through his hair. The others gratefully followed his example. The masks might look cool, but they itched something chronic.

"Are you Lyudmila?" JD continued, his hand hovering over the handle of his sword.

The girl wasn't showing any signs of possession. No twitching. No black eyes. She was about the same age as JD, of mixed heritage with light brown skin and a short bob that framed her face. Cute in that geek-girl sort of way. She wore tracksuit bottoms and a bright purple hoodie.

"Milly," the girl said quietly. "The only person who calls me Lyudmila is my mother. At least, she used to…"

JD didn't need her to carry on. They'd listened to the FaceTime with her friend and the panicked phone call to the police after Niv had hacked her accounts.

"Okay, Milly," Tom said, stepping closer, and resting a gentle hand on the girl's elbow. "Everything is going to be okay."

The girl's face hardened. "Really? Really!" She shook off Tom's arm. "I just saw my mother's manager make her stab her PA in the heart. How exactly is that okay?"

"I know this is all seriously strange," Tom said, looking slightly shaken that his usual charm hadn't worked. "Believe me, we all know. But for now, we need to get you out of here. Is there somewhere safe you can go?"

"What? No. I've only been in Chicago a few months. My mother—" She choked before she could finish the sentence.

JD took a deep breath. Usually it was left to Gail to explain things like this. Or Tom would just hypnotise them.

"That's not your mother any more."

"What do you mean?" She looked pallid, like she might be sick any minute.

"She's a demon," Connor said, appearing from the kitchen. He was still wearing his mask. "Hey, you've taken your masks off. No fair." He pulled his off and immediately replaced it with his red snapback.

"Way with the sensitivity, Con," Zek said, glaring at him.

Niv clipped the Irish boy around the back of his head, knocking his tatty cap to the floor again.

"What?" Connor said, rubbing at his hair. "She asked."

Milly stared blankly at JD. "A demon?"

He nodded.

"A demon?" she said again.

"Yes," JD said. "Demon."

"Come on. Is this like some weird reality TV show?"

"No, fighting demons is our job."

"Fighting demons? Running around with swords?" She gestured at the weapon in JD's hands. "But you're a...a boy band." Milly stared at them all. "This has to be a joke."

"Does that look like a joke?" JD said, pointing to the body.

Milly looked like he'd slapped her. She covered her mouth with her hand. "No, no it doesn't. Poor Alice. I should have done something...I should have done anything."

JD knew how she felt.

"There was nothing you could have done," said Tom. "You were right to message us."

Niv dragged his index and middle finger across the back of his left wrist.

"What?" JD said.

"The police? Yeah, I called them too," Milly said.

"They'll be here soon," Connor said. "We have to go, like now."

Niv pushed his brother aside and pointed at Milly, his brow creased. Then, his palms open and facing each other, he made rotating circular movements with his hands.

"Yes. My father was deaf."

"What's going on?" JD said.

"Um, I think Milly may know sign language," Zek said.

Niv started signing frantically, a huge grin on his face.

"Whoa, slow down," Milly said. "Can you repeat that? I'm a bit out of practice."

Niv did, slower this time.

"Well, it's not really amazing. I think sign language should be taught in all schools."

Niv threw his hands up in the air and nodded like a bobble-headed dog. He signed again, shaking his head and pointing at Zek.

"But, if your brother doesn't understand it then..."

"Ha ha," Zek said, grabbing his brother's hands. "Of course I understand it. Niv is just messing with you, aren't you, Niv?" He fixed his brother with a stern glare.

JD didn't know what was going on between Zek and Niv, but he was suddenly embarrassed. He knew the odd word that Niv signed, but he'd never bothered to learn properly, he just relied on Zek to do all the translating. And yet this girl could understand his friend perfectly.

"We don't have time for this," JD said. "The police are on their way and we need to leave. Here's how it's going to go. When they get here, you say you heard screaming and locked yourself in your room. You tell them you saw nothing and heard nothing. Then you're going to go and stay with someone and not come back here."

Milly dropped the bat. "You're going to leave me?" She looked at Tom. JD could practically hear Tom's heart melting.

"Maybe we don't have—" Tom started.

"Yes we do." JD cut him off. He and Tom stared at each other, a conversation as silent and yet as flowing as Niv's going on between the two of them. They knew each other so well that they didn't need words to make themselves understood.

"But she's seen us," Tom said finally.

JD looked back at the girl. Could they trust her to keep their secret?

Niv tapped his shoulder and showed him a read-out on his phone. The police car was at the top of the road. They had two minutes to get out. He'd have to take the chance. Even if she told, who would believe her? He pulled his mask and goggles back on and turned to go.

"Wait," the girl said.

JD felt himself tense.

"Maybe…I can be useful?"

"I don't mean to be rude—" JD said, without turning around.

"But you're going to be anyway," Zek muttered.

JD ignored Zek and turned back to face the girl. "But exactly what use could you be?"

"I have information. I heard them talking."

Niv tapped at his wrist. They had less than a minute

before the police arrived.

"Go on."

"I'll tell you on one condition." She paused, looking from boy to boy. "You take me with you."

JD stared at the girl through his goggles. She was small, her hair was a mess and her eyes were red from crying, but she looked determined.

He heard the *whoop-whoop* of a police car. He had to make his mind up now. Leave her here and take the chance she could blow their cover? Take her and risk her finding out even more about them? He knew what Gail would do.

"Okay, but we leave now."

"My phone," she said. "I must have dropped it upstairs."

"No time." He grabbed her wrist and pulled her out the door. The boys followed close behind.

"Where are we going?" Milly said as he bundled her into the jeep.

"Agatha," Tom said, sliding into the seat next to her.

JD jumped into the passenger seat with Connor beside him as the twins squeezed in the back.

Blue lights flashed. The police were almost here.

"Who's Agatha?" she said.

"Just you wait," Connor said, slamming the jeep into reverse and hitting the accelerator. "You're gonna love her."

I cried all night

"Welcome aboard," Tom said, showing Milly onto the bus.

The first thing that hit Milly was the smell. Unsurprising really, given five boys lived here. She hadn't been in too many boys' bedrooms in her time, but she had been shoved into the boys' locker rooms in one of her schools and this didn't smell that different. Sweaty socks, deodorant and musty damp.

"Um, wait here," Tom said, holding up a finger and stopping her from going any further. He ran down the aisle, pulling discarded underpants off the seats and kicking shoes under the bunk beds at the back of the bus. He turned around and faced her from the end of the aisle, his cheeks tinged pink. "Sorry, we're not used to company."

"It's lovely," Milly said, taking in the interior. The bus was lined with dark wood and tan leather and, other than the mess, looked more like a yacht than a bus. There were four flat-screen TVs lined up on one wall; game consoles; speaker systems. Three electric guitars rested on the sofas and a keyboard was built into the countertop. It was every teenage boy's dream.

"It's our home from home," Connor said, grabbing hold of a bar and starting to do chin-ups.

JD hadn't said much on the journey here but Milly had felt his annoyance the whole way. He made Milly feel so awkward; too aware of what she was wearing or what her hair was doing. She found herself fussing at her messy fringe every time he bothered to look her way. He was so different to Tom, who was doing his best to make her feel at ease.

"Can I get you anything, Milly?" Tom asked, leading her to a comfortable chair and encouraging her to sit down. "A drink? Food? We have pretty much anything you can imagine." Tom had stuck by Milly's side since they'd left the house and she was glad of it.

"No thanks, I'm…"

She was going to say fine, but that seemed so wrong. She kept expecting to break down any second. But for now, all she felt was dazed. Like none of this was real. Maybe that was because it *was* all a dream and she would wake up from it any moment. That would make sense. Because a world-famous boy band turning up and saving her from demons did not.

"You must be Lyudmila."

She looked up to see a tall woman walking down the aisle of the bus towards her. The woman had a glittering eyepatch and short hair, shaved on one side and longer on the other, and glowing, ebony skin. Her one visible eye was ringed in heavy eyeliner and she wore skinny black jeans and a baggy black vest that revealed a purple lotus flower tattoo across her shoulder. She must have been at least Milly's mother's age, but there was something youthful about the way she carried herself, despite the walking stick.

"Milly. Most people call me Milly."

"I'm Gail." She reached out a hand covered in silver rings. Milly took it, expecting a handshake, but instead Gail pulled her into a tight hug.

"It's okay," she said. "You're safe now."

The temptation to stay in that hug and cry and cry was so strong, but Milly forced herself to push away. If she started crying now, she didn't think she would ever stop.

Gail gave her a last squeeze that seemed to say the hug would still be there when she needed it and let Milly go. "Welcome to our home. Excuse the mess – I sleep at the back, the boys sleep in this pigsty." She waved around at the bus. "I have taught them to fight demons but apparently tidying up after themselves would take a miracle."

"Um, yeah, about that…" Milly said.

"Of course, you must have a lot of questions," Gail said, gesturing for Milly to take a seat.

She was grateful to take the weight off her shaking legs. "I don't even know where to start. I guess, well, what *are* demons?"

"Good question. In religious texts they're seen as evil spirits or fallen angels. Some scholars referred to them as the embodiment of all that is dark in humanity. Those of us who have to fight the things? All we know for sure is that they come from a place called the Netherworld."

"The demon dimension," Connor chipped in.

"It's said there was a time when humans and demons lived side by side, in relative harmony. But it wasn't long before the demons tried to enslave humanity. The humans fought back using powerful magic long since forgotten, which blasted the demons out of their bodies and sent their spirits back to the Netherworld."

"Pow!" Connor said, miming blasting an energy ball out of his hands.

"That's why they have no physical form of their own in the human world," Tom said. "They look like shadows. For demons to operate here, they have to possess a human host."

"Like my mother?"

Tom nodded.

"So is there a way to get the demon out of her? Like, an exorcism or something?"

Milly watched as the boys and Gail all looked from one to another.

JD was the only one willing to speak. "Your mother is dead."

"JD!" Tom and Gail said in unison.

"What? She needs to know. What's the point in wasting any more time?"

"What JD is trying so very badly to explain", Tom said, "is that the moment the demon took over your mother's body, her…well I guess what you might call her soul, was lost. And once a demon takes possession there's no coming back."

Milly covered her face with her hands. She remembered watching that black smoke invade her mother. She'd known then really, even if she wasn't willing to believe it, that her mother was dead.

"Aliens," she muttered through her hands.

"What?" Zek asked.

Milly dropped her hands and looked up. "I thought she'd been taken over by aliens."

"I wish," Connor said, launching himself into the air and landing on a nearby sofa. "Aliens would be well cool."

Niv clipped him around the back of the head.

"So demons are real and they go around possessing people?" Milly said, pushing down her grief and focusing on the facts. "But why?"

"What do you mean?" Tom asked.

"I mean why? What do they want?"

"The same thing many humans want," Gail said. "Power.

Some believe…" Gail hesitated, as if not sure that Milly was ready to hear everything. "Some believe that they're trying to find a way to get back to our world. To finish what they started before and enslave humanity."

"Never going to happen," JD said, opening a fridge and pulling out a bottle of water.

"You sure about that, Jay?" Zek said, grabbing the water out of JD's hands so he had to get a second one.

"Deadly sure," he said, twisting the lid off the bottle. "Because we'll stop them."

"Damn straight we will!" Connor said, holding his hand up for a high five. JD left him hanging.

"So that's what you do?" Milly asked. "You…fight demons?"

"We try," Tom said.

Milly looked from boy to boy, shaking her head. "But… but why you? Isn't there, like, a department for demon-killing?"

"That's not a bad idea," Zek said. "We should set it up. And get badges – I've always wanted badges."

"Because adults are too easily corrupted by demons," Tom said. "Too susceptible to promises of fame or fortune. Most adults, anyway." He smiled at Gail.

"When it comes to going up against evil, the more pure-hearted the person, the better chance they have of withstanding the demonic influence."

"Okay then, but the boy band?"

"We needed a cover," Tom said. "An excuse to travel all around the world, following the trails left by demons."

"Plus, the money is useful," Zek said, looking at his perfectly manicured nails. "There's not much money in demon hunting. So it was either boy band or international jewel thieves. I voted for thieves but I got overruled."

Milly sat back in her seat. None of this made any kind of sense. But she had left sense behind, along with the rest of her life. "This is crazy, you realize that? Completely and utterly crazy."

The boys winced.

"What?" Milly asked, realizing she'd said something wrong.

"We try not to use the word 'crazy' around here," Tom said, looking over at Gail.

"That's okay," Gail said, smiling softly. "Now, Milly, it's our turn for questions."

"Oh, yes, right." The only reason they'd agreed to take her with them. "What do you want to know?"

"Start by telling us about your mother."

Milly took a deep steadying breath. She could feel the tears and rage threatening to break through, and she willed them away. For now, she was going to focus on what was in front of her. "Where to start? She is…I mean, I guess, she *was* an opera singer. She used to be a pretty big deal.

The lead soprano for the Opéra de Paris, jetting all over the world. She met my dad in London, had me and just kept going. Berlin, Sydney, New York. Then when Dad died she had to look after me on her own. Well, it wasn't easy for her." Milly swallowed hard, trying to fight back the pressure of tears in her throat. "The jobs stopped coming, the phones stopped ringing. She managed to get a few chorus jobs at the English National Opera, till she had another falling out with the director. Then she got a new manager and things started to change."

"What do you know about this manager?"

"Absolutely nothing except his name: Mourdant."

"The demon dude in the silver suit?" Zek said.

"That's him."

"And he knew us," JD said.

"What do you mean?" Gail turned to face JD.

"He said that he'd been watching us, that he offered you some deal that you refused."

"Wait, silver suits? Does he wear sunglasses indoors?"

"Ding-ding-ding! That's the scumbag," Zek said.

"I…I had no idea he was a demon. I thought he was just a creep manager trying to get a slice of the action. How could I have missed that?"

"He was seriously powerful. Like, boss-level powerful," Zek said.

"Hmm," Gail said, clearly annoyed with herself. "Now,

Milly, I need you to tell us everything about your mother's possession."

"I...don't know what I saw. I was so scared. And I think the champagne Mourdant gave me might have been drugged. It's all so foggy."

"Try your hardest to remember."

Milly took another deep breath and relayed what had happened as best she could, describing the way Mourdant had forced her mother to stab Alice, how she had carved something into her own arm...

"That symbol was to give the demon permission to possess her," Gail said.

Milly rubbed at her own arm in the place her mother had carved the mark, just above her wrist. "I don't think she knew what she was doing, not really."

"They never do," JD said.

"But if the symbol was all Mourdant needed, then why kill Alice?"

"Some more powerful summonings require a sacrifice in order to bind the demon soul to the body. Often demons use animals: chickens, goats and the like. But when they want to summon something *really* powerful, well..."

Milly swallowed down the bile that rose in her throat. How could her mother have agreed to this? Even though she'd tried to stop it when it came to it, she must have known what was at stake. Milly knew she had been desperate to become famous again, but she hadn't realized just how desperate.

"What happened, after the possession?" Gail said.

"She was…different. And so was Mourdant. Before, he'd been the one calling the shots, but after he got down on his knees and bowed to her. Called her Zyanya, Priestess of Tes…" Milly racked her brain, trying to remember the word. "Tescat something. I didn't understand the word, but it gave me the serious creeps." Milly wrapped her arms around her body. It was warm in the bus, but she couldn't stop shivering.

"A demon priestess," Tom said. "That…that doesn't sound good."

"Let's not get carried away," Gail said. "Milly said herself she wasn't sure what she heard."

"She also said she had information," JD snapped, "and she's hardly told us anything useful."

"I…I'm sorry, I can't remember," Milly said. Up until now, the boys had looked confident, cocky even. The fearful looks on their faces were starting to scare her.

"She's told us more than enough for tonight," Gail said, fixing JD with a meaningful stare. "We'll talk more in the morning after some rest. It's" – she checked her watch – "damn, it's already morning. Okay, Niv, check the police report from tonight and make sure there's no mention of Milly. While she's with us, she's a ghost. Complete scrubbing of her name from all databases. We can't have the police looking for her."

Niv positioned a keyboard in front of him and started typing.

"We'll get back on the trail tomorrow. I'll push back the meeting with the tech company, and see what I can do about the photo shoot with the coconut water people, but I can't cancel the radio interview. Milly, make yourself at home. I'll be in the room in the back if you need me. And, boys, I know I don't need to tell you about how we treat guests. Especially female ones." She gave each of the boys a withering stare.

"No, ma'am," they all said in unison.

"Okay." Gail squeezed Milly's arm as she passed, then vanished through a door at the back of the bus.

"Night," Milly said quietly.

"Itabenice," Connor said through a massive yawn and sounding like a howling dog, "to have just one night off from saving the world, you know?"

"You think someone else is going to stop whatever's going on here?" JD said. "I'm sorry it's not all half-pipes and ollies, Connor, this is our life. No pretending it isn't."

"No pretending you don't like it, either," Milly said, louder than she had intended. The boys all looked at her with a mix of shock and amusement on their faces. Normally she would have backed down. Said sorry and let it go. But she was beyond worrying about what boys like JD might think of her. "Come on, you're telling me you don't get off on this? Charging around with swords, playing at being heroes?"

JD's jaw clenched so hard Milly could hear his teeth grinding. "We're not *playing* at anything."

"Could have fooled me," she muttered under her breath.

"I'm sorry that we bothered risking our lives to save you."

"I didn't mean that," Milly said, realizing how ungrateful she had sounded. "It's just…"

"It's okay, Milly," Tom said. "You don't need to explain. This must all seem so unbelievable to you."

"Besides," Connor said, "you're right. It is fun! Amiright?" He stretched out an arm and waited for a high five from JD.

JD stood up and grabbed his mask and goggles.

"Where're you off to?" Tom said, moving to block JD's path.

"Just out."

"Sure," Tom said disbelievingly.

"I can't sleep right now. Besides," he said, glancing over his shoulder at Milly, "it's a little crowded in here."

And before anyone could say another word, JD pushed Tom aside and slammed the door of the bus behind him.

"What was that about?" Connor asked the group.

"Don't worry about it," Tom said. "It's been a long night for us all. Let's try and get a few hours' sleep and we can work out what to do tomorrow."

"Which is now," Zek said, looking at his watch.

Milly checked her own. It was 2.46 a.m. Her body ached and her eyes itched, but her mind was buzzing.

"You can sleep in my bunk," Tom said, pointing at one of the beds. "I'll take the sofa." Milly started to protest – she'd never so much as had a slumber party at a boy's house before and the idea of sleeping in Tom's bed made her stomach flutter. But Tom held up his hand. "The sheets are clean and seriously, you'll be doing me a favour. Connor snores." He gestured with his thumb at the messy-haired drummer, who had leaped up into his bed.

"I do not!"

Niv's hands moved in a blur and his twin brother snorted with laughter.

"What? What did he say?" Connor asked.

"He said you're so loud that it keeps the demons away," Milly said.

Niv put his finger to his lips.

"Oh, sorry, was I not meant to translate that?"

"Damn," Zek said. "We're going to have to be careful about insulting Connor all the time with you around, Milly."

"Ha! I'm going to get Milly to teach me sign language, seeing as you've always said you can't teach me."

"It's not that I can't teach you, Con," Zek said. "It's that I *choose* not to. It's more fun this way."

Connor threw his sock in Zek's face.

Tom unzipped the black overalls he'd been wearing to reveal a T-shirt with a faded red donkey on it and toned arms with a black tattoo of a five-pointed star on one. He paused before completely removing the overalls, catching Milly's eye.

"Oh, sorry, yes," she said, spinning around to avoid watching him undress – only to be faced with Zek, who was now in his underwear. Zek didn't seem to mind, but Milly's face was burning. This was going to be awkward. She settled it by closing her eyes.

She felt a hand on her shoulder. "It's okay, we're decent," Tom said.

"As decent as we shall ever be," Zek said, flashing Milly a playful wink.

They were enjoying her discomfort a lot more than she was, that much was clear.

"Here," Zek said, throwing a black T-shirt at Milly. She held it out to see it had SLEIGH written on it in gold lettering. "Keep it. There was a mix-up at the printer's and we have hundreds of them to get rid of."

"Thanks," she said. "Um, where's the loo?"

Tom pointed to a door at the end of the bus, opposite the one Gail had walked through.

When she returned, the boys were already in their bunks. Milly lay down on the bed. There was no way she was going to be able to sleep. Not with the ache in her heart and the buzzing in her brain. All the things that she had worried about – fitting in at school, the pressure of expectation from her mother – none of it mattered any more. She was alone. Well, apart from five boys from the most famous boy band in the world.

Milly was used to fame. She'd spent her whole life in the shadow of her mother and she'd seen what it cost. Not just the hours and hours it took to hone your talent, but your privacy, your personal life. Even your soul, it seemed. And these boys were risking still more than that. From the way they talked, they'd obviously faced monsters like the ones she'd seen tonight before. So frequently, it seemed, they were able to make jokes about it. Did that make them cool or cold? Milly didn't know.

JD was the one who bothered her most of all. She guessed there was something going on behind the snapping and moody stares, but she had enough of her own problems to deal with right now without having to worry about what was up with him.

She wriggled in the bunk, trying to get comfortable, wishing for the escape of sleep. Her father had always said, *The brightest mornings follow the darkest nights.*

As the sounds of Connor's snoring blended with the rattling of a train overhead, Milly knew deep in her heart that nothing would ever be easy again. And finally, she let the tears come.

Tell me your secrets

JD sat on the steps outside the bus, listening to the ebb and flow of Connor's snoring from inside. He'd become so used to it now, it rarely bothered him. Just like all the annoying things the rest of his bandmates did: Zek and his constant sarcasm and inability to take anything seriously. Niv's habit of tapping his pencil on the desk for hours at a time. Even Tom's perky optimism, which used to drive JD mad when they first met, now only made him roll his eyes. But currently, there was only one person disturbing his peace. Milly.

JD knew he shouldn't be annoyed by her. She hadn't done anything other than lose someone to a demon, just like the rest of them. And that was JD's problem. In so many ways, she *was* just like the rest of them. JD had seen how Gail hugged the girl, like she'd found another stray. And the way Tom looked at her. It made him feel…uneasy.

JD didn't want the girl joining them. He was settled now with the four other boys and Gail. They were a family, which was the only thing JD had ever wished for. It had been those two words he put on every birthday and Christmas list from when he could write till the day Gail turned up. A family. For some reason that he couldn't explain, he felt that Milly was going to disturb that.

"Don't be stupid," JD said to himself. "She's only here for the night and she'll be gone tomorrow."

And yet, he didn't know how he felt about her leaving either. Irritated at how petty he was being, JD stood up, determined to go back inside and try to get some sleep. He might even have a word with Milly and apologize, if she was still awake.

He stopped for a moment before opening the door and watched the moon breaking out from behind thick clouds. It was a full moon, sharpening the shadows around him. JD liked the darkness and hiding in the shadows a lot more than he liked standing in the limelight. And he often worried about how much of a kick he got out of hunting demons. He'd never admitted that to anyone. Not even Tom and he told Tom everything. After each mission, he worried about it even more. There was something wrong with him, he knew, and he was terrified that someone would find out.

Milly had come close to it earlier when she'd accused JD of getting off on it all. Perhaps that's why the girl unsettled him so much. She'd seen straight through him after less than an hour.

Anxiety coiled in his stomach again, destroying all thoughts of sleep. He slumped back against the side of the bus, going over tonight's mission in his mind, trying to work out what he could have done differently. How he'd managed to let not one but two demons escape. Well, maybe the hunt wasn't over yet.

He pulled out his phone. "DAD, access headcam footage from…say, an hour ago."

"Accessing," DAD's automated voice said.

The footage of Milly's house appeared on screen. "Fast forward." It scanned through their arrival; them smashing through the doors and seeing the two demons for the first time. "Stop," JD said, and the screen paused on a perfect shot of Mourdant as he came down the stairs. "Grab that. Run it through the database, cross-referenced with the name Mourdant."

DAD had access to systems no civilian should be able to access: police databases, the intranets of newspapers and even land registry files. The screen flashed and a moment later a professional photo of Mourdant's smug face appeared on screen. If it hadn't been for worrying he might damage his phone, JD would have punched it.

There was information about the guy's business, the people he represented, a police report investigating tax evasion and there, at the bottom of the report, an address. JD smiled.

He walked around to the back of the bus, flipped open a keypad and punched in a number. Machinery whirred and a panel in Agatha's side slid open. Behind it were five motorbikes, one for each of the boys. JD's was a black Triumph Bonneville. Modelled on Steve McQueen's bike in *The Great Escape*, it looked like something from the fifties but it bristled with the latest tech and extra modifications, such as a side holster for his sword. He wheeled it away from Agatha and onto the broken tarmac of the road. Black helmet on and GPS coordinates loaded into the satnav, he swung his leg over the hand-stitched seat and thumbed the ignition. Five minutes later he was roaring down the highway and into the dark.

He twisted the throttle back, the front wheel of the bike rearing in response, and sped on. Cutting through the Victorian-era buildings of Old Town, he headed for the lake. The coast of Lake Michigan was so vast and it stretched out so far into the distance that JD kept forgetting it wasn't the sea, but in fact Chicago was over 700 miles from the ocean. He wove along North Lake Shore Drive, the soothing empty blackness of the water on his left, the glowing high-rises of the city on his right. The road led him over the Chicago River and he took a sharp right, his knee brushing the ground as he leaned into the corner, heading away from the coast now and following the snaking waterway through the heart of the city. The streets were mostly empty apart from taxis taking people home. A party boat floated up the river, lights flashing and music booming. Up ahead he saw the building he was heading for – a glass skyscraper that towered over the city, built in three sections that extended out and out, reminding JD of a huge walkie-talkie complete with aerial.

It made perfect sense that Mourdant would live here: one of the most exclusive addresses in Chicago. That also meant getting in might be a problem. There would be a concierge at least, possibly even security. But JD had been trained to get around such things.

He pulled up outside the building, and strolled in through the front door like he owned the place.

A doorman wearing a purple suit and gloves tipped his hat in welcome. JD walked up to the reception desk and smiled his best boy-band smile.

The woman behind the desk had black hair scraped back across her head and fixed in a fierce bun. She peered at him over thick black glasses and for a moment looked like she was about to object to his presence. Then recognition hit.

"Hi, sorry, I know it's late," JD said. "I'm still on UK time."

"Oh, no…no problem at all. How can I help?" Her cheeks and neck were flushed.

Perfect, JD thought, *a fan.*

He leaned over the desk, closing the distance between them. She did the same, so that their heads were only a few centimetres apart. "It's a bit delicate, Barbra," he said, reading the name off her badge, "but I know I can trust you. I'm here for a meeting with Mourdant to discuss the possibility of new representation. But I can't have it on record that I was here. I am sure you understand, the press can be so..." He stared deep into her eyes. "Intrusive."

"Oh, yes, I completely understand. I'll just call up."

It seemed he didn't need Tom's hypnotic powers to bring this woman under his spell. He placed his hand over hers as she reached for the phone. "No, I can't even trust that his phone hasn't been tapped."

The woman's eyes widened in delight. She was loving the drama. "Oh, my, well yes, one hears such things."

"You can only imagine, Barbra."

"Imagine...yes."

"So if you could just buzz me up? He's expecting me."

"No problem. And if there's anything else you need..."

"He's on the eixty-felth, right?" JD said, intentionally mumbling the number.

"Sixty-seventh, yes. Apartment number 236."

JD winked. "Thanks, you've been a doll."

Barbra giggled and flushed even redder.

The elevator doors pinged open and JD walked straight in. JD might not always like being in the limelight, but he couldn't deny fame did have its advantages.

Arriving on the sixty-seventh, JD stopped outside number 236 and listened. It was silent. He slid a pack of picks out of his back pocket and got to work. The door clicked and swung open.

The apartment was illuminated by the lights outside streaming in through the glass windows. JD could see the river glittering below and the black expanse that was Lake Michigan in the distance. There was the barest amount of furniture and what little there was looked designed to achieve maximum style and minimum comfort.

JD crept from room to room, checking Mourdant wasn't here. Once he was sure he was alone, he started looking for anything that might help him track Mourdant down. The place was completely empty, not so much as a coffee mug or a magazine to suggest that anyone lived here. JD moved through the living room, peering through doorways till he found what he assumed must be the master bedroom. The bed hadn't been slept in. The wardrobes were filled with a row of identical silver suits. But something else inside the wardrobe caught JD's attention. A faint line in the plaster.

JD pushed and, to his surprise and delight, the wall shifted.

Behind it was a small room. He found the light switch and flicked it. Whereas the rest of the apartment was clean and sparse, this space was rammed and filthy. A small desk in the corner was piled high with books, crumpled papers littered the floor and three of the walls were scrawled with red demonic symbols. JD covered his nose with the back of his hand to ward off the stench. He didn't want to think about what those symbols had been painted with.

The fourth wall was covered in pinned pictures of people and articles torn out of newspapers from all over the world. Some of the photos had lines through them, but two were circled. The first showed an image of a young Japanese man holding a trophy. The other was a picture of a woman JD recognized. He peered closer. He'd only caught a glimpse of her earlier, but she was unmistakable. It was Milly's mother. In the picture she was dressed like a Viking woman, with battle armour and long golden braids. At the bottom Mourdant had written and underlined, "*Host???*"

JD moved to the desk and riffled through the papers. He pulled out a sheet of parchment and knocked something to the floor. A thick notebook bound in red leather. JD picked it up and unwound the string holding it closed before flicking through the pages.

Most of the contents had been written in a language JD didn't understand, but he could make out dates, which started in 1982. Some of the pages had been scratched through and words like *Failure* and *Disaster* had been written over them in English. Whatever Mourdant had been planning went back years.

The final pages in the diary were covered in black marks that weren't even in an alphabet he recognized. In the flickering light they looked like an army of dancing ants. As he looked closer, the marks took form. Triangles. Rows of lines. Small drawings of animals. His finger hovered over one symbol that seemed to call to him: a looping circle with overlapping ends. The same symbol he'd seen on the arms of the demons they had fought in the motel. JD couldn't read the words but he knew what he was looking at. A ritual.

He turned the final page over and written in neat, sharp writing on the back was one word…

I say your name (in my sleep)

"Tezcatlipoca!" Milly woke, gasping for breath. She'd been dreaming about her mother – trapped somewhere, screaming for help. But no matter how hard Milly tried, she couldn't get there before a great blackness consumed her, sucking her down and down. She'd tried calling out but no sound escaped. And then the name she'd heard the demon priestess Zyanya say came back to her, twisting her stomach and bursting out of her.

Her brow dripped with sweat and her throat was raw, whether from the crying or the silent screams she didn't know. She needed a glass of water. She wiped her eyes with the neck of her borrowed T-shirt and clambered out of the bunk. Four of the boys were sleeping soundly: Connor still snoring, Niv and Zek totally indistinguishable now they were both silent, Tom curled up on the sofa, looking serene, his mop of light hair falling over his face. JD still hadn't returned. Milly felt strangely guilty. She knew he hadn't wanted to bring her with them and she wished she hadn't sounded so ungrateful earlier. But it wasn't as if he was making any of this easy for her.

She padded in her socks towards the kitchenette. Unwashed plates, crumpled-up serviettes and three old pizza boxes lay scattered around. She picked up a knife and used it to push the boxes and paper napkins into the trash can. It seemed the boys were too busy saving the world from demons to worry about washing up.

She tried a few of the cupboards before finding a glass. She felt a sudden pang of loss for her favourite glass at home – the one with a moustache printed on it. She'd found it in a second-hand shop in London with Naledi and had smothered it in bubble wrap when she'd packed for the move to Chicago. Now it was left behind in the house along with everything else she owned. JD had dragged her away before she'd had a chance to get any of her things. How petty to be thinking about *objects* with everything that had happened. It was like her brain wouldn't let her deal with the impossibility of what she'd seen, so it focused on the little, stupid, menial things instead.

The water was ice-cold and soothed her throat. But she didn't want to risk going back to sleep just yet; the nightmare was still too fresh. She filled the glass up again, sat down at the table, pulled her knees up under her chin and thought.

In a handful of hours her life had unravelled and she couldn't see a way to put it right.

The bus shook as an L train rumbled above. Milly wondered who would be riding it at this time of the morning. Did demons take the L train? she wondered dumbly. How many demons were there out there, passing as human? She thought back to all the weird people she'd met in her life, all the strange artists and hangers-on her mother used to attract. Had any of them been demons? How could she trust anything any more? There was a world she never knew existed and she'd been thrown right into the heart of it.

She knew two things. One: she didn't want to go back to the house – not yet, maybe not ever. Two: she wanted revenge for her mother. She was going to make Mourdant and the demon he had summoned pay for what they had done. The problem was, how? She was just a teenager with straight As but no idea about how to fight demons. The boys, on the other hand, were armed and clearly knew how to handle themselves. She needed them. But JD had made it quite clear that they didn't need her. If she was going to be allowed to stick around, she was going to have to make herself useful. She couldn't fight, but there was one thing she could do. Study.

She patted her back pocket, expecting her phone to be there, then remembered it was back at the house. There was a laptop on the table. She pulled it towards her and was relieved to see it didn't have a lock on it. She opened the internet browser and keyed one word into the search bar: *Tezcatlipoca*.

Even looking at the word made her blood go cold. There were pages of results and the more she read, the more afraid she became. She found a pencil and a notepad and began scribbling down notes as she went. Just wait till she told them all what she'd found.

Just go

JD slammed open the door of the bus, not caring if anyone inside was still sleeping.

"Wha—? Ouch!" Connor sat up so fast he hit his head on the ceiling.

JD charged down the aisle, ignoring the protests from the stirring boys, and stopped at the table, where a red-eyed Milly sat, scribbling into a notebook.

"What's going on, JD?" Tom asked, sitting up on the sofa and scratching his curls.

Zek and Niv were fully awake now, long legs dangling over the edge of their bunks, looking at him with tired yet curious eyes.

JD threw Mourdant's diary on the table in front of Milly and beamed. "I know what Mourdant is up to. He's trying to bring back…Tezli…Tezli…" He struggled to pronounce the name he'd read.

"Tezcatlipoca," Milly said, stifling a yawn.

"Tezliwhatnow?" Connor said.

JD's smile froze. "But…how?"

"Could one of you tell us what's going on?" Tom said, struggling to untangle himself from a blanket.

Milly looked to JD as if asking for permission. He shrugged. This girl had a way of stealing his thunder.

"I finally remembered the name I heard Zyanya say and I looked it up. Tezcatlipoca was the Aztec god of death, shadows and…" She spun the laptop around, showing Tom one of the pages she'd been reading.

"Demons," Tom said, scanning the page.

"Whoa," Connor said. "A god of demons. That's heavy."

"Do demons even have gods?" Zek asked.

Niv shrugged.

"Whatever he's up to, Mourdant has been planning this for years," JD said, picking the diary up and flicking to the front page. "I think he tried some kind of ritual dedicated to Tezlico…" He hesitated again.

"How about we just call him the Big T, okay?" Tom said.

"Dedicated to the Big T, but it failed. He needed the priestess, this Zyanya."

"And thanks to my mother," Milly said, "now he has her."

"This is not so good," Connor said.

"We're talking about a god of demons here, Con," Zek said. "'Not so good' doesn't come close. We're talking 'end of the world as we know it'."

"I go to bed for what feels like a matter of minutes and you're talking about the end of the world." Gail walked out of her room, yawning. Her hair was stuck up on one side and she wasn't wearing her eyepatch, revealing the scarred skin around her injured eye socket. "What's going on?"

"I went to Mourdant's apartment to do some digging and—"

"You went there alone?" Tom said.

Gail sucked her teeth. "JD, how many times do I need to tell—"

"Rule one: never go alone. We're a team, no man is an island, blah blah blah. I get it, all right? Do you want to hear what I found or not?"

Gail nodded reluctantly.

"Mourdant's diary. I can't make most of it out, but this seems pretty clear." JD picked up the leather-bound book and turned it to the last page before handing it over to Gail.

"Hmm, it's definitely a ritual of some kind. Maybe a sacrifice to the god in return for something."

"Can I see?" Milly asked. And before JD could object, Gail handed it over to the girl. She flicked through the pages. "It's not a language I know, but this bit he's scribbled and circled is in Latin."

"You know Latin?" Tom said.

"Some. And French, obviously, as my mother is...I mean she was French."

Niv signed.

"Yeah, and sign language," Milly said, signing at Niv as she spoke.

"Right now, I don't care if she knows Elvish," JD said. "Can we focus on the diary? What does it say?"

"I do know Elvish," Milly muttered, before coughing and looking back down at the diary. "It's hard to read his writing. Fica? No, *Sica. Sica Umbrarum. Umbrarum* means shadow, like in umbra physics, and *Sica* is, um…knife. No, blade. Blade of shadows. Wait, Mourdant mentioned a blade. He said he had tracked it down and that once it had been returned to Zyanya nothing would be able to stop her."

JD blinked at Milly. Was this girl for real? She'd only found out about the demon world a matter of hours ago and she was already proving herself essential.

"The rest of the writing on the page, I'm sorry, I don't even recognize the alphabet."

"Run it through the translator," JD said, taking the diary off Milly and handing it over to Niv.

Niv lay the diary on a scanner and pressed a few buttons. A moment later a message flashed up on screen.

NOT RECOGNIZED

"We need more information."

"Maybe this professor could help?" Milly said, flicking

through a notebook she had covered in scribbles. "Professor of Aztec Studies at Chicago University."

"I guess it's worth a shot," JD said. Milly seemed to be one step ahead of him again.

"The radio interview is at ten. We leave at nine," Gail said. "Now I'm going back to bed."

The boys fought over who got to use the shower first; Tom wanted to know where Connor had hidden his boots; and all the while Milly sat there, looking at JD, her expression unreadable. Anger? Disappointment? Fear? He couldn't tell. All he knew was that when he looked at Milly, he felt like he'd failed somehow. In not killing Mourdant or saving her mother from possession. In not being able to save her from all of this. Tom pushed him out of the way so he could get to his boots, which were apparently under the table. When he straightened up he looked from JD to Milly and back again. Tom shook his head only the smallest of fractions, but JD knew what it meant. *Let up on her.*

Tom turned back to Milly. "You need to borrow some clothes, Milly?"

The girl looked down at the baggy tracksuit bottoms she'd been wearing since they first met her. "Actually, that would be great."

"Just don't let him give you one of his horrible sweaters,"

Connor shouted from the front of the bus, where he was doing chin-ups again.

"I'll have you know they are vintage," Tom said, brushing imaginary dust off his black and green striped top.

"Yeah, vintage as in dead people's. And they should have been buried with them," Zek said.

Tom stuck his tongue out at Zek, before sliding a drawer out from the wall. After rummaging around for a bit he pulled out a T-shirt and a pair of jeans. "Will this be okay?" The T-shirt had a picture of a cat shooting laser beams out of its eyes. "I, um, I went through a phase of buying 'so bad they're good' tees."

"So bad they should be burned," Zek said, stretching.

"They're perfect, thanks," Milly said. "Not like I'm one to talk." She gestured towards her clothing.

"You look great," Tom said.

JD could tell by the way his eyes widened that he instantly regretted it.

Judging by Zek's chuckle, he wasn't the only one who noticed. JD couldn't hear exactly what the twin muttered, but it sounded something like, "Slick."

Milly smiled. "Thanks, those are great. You're…I mean, thanks."

JD could have sworn he saw Tom blush as he handed over the clothes. "They'll be too big on you, but I'm sure you'll make it work," Tom said, giving Milly his bright, goofy smile.

When he turned away to get dressed, JD was pretty sure Tom avoided his eye.

The sooner we get to the bottom of this demon god stuff, JD thought, the sooner that girl is out of here.

Number one fan

It had taken just under an hour to drive across the city to the University of Chicago campus. Fifty bumpy minutes in a bus full of bickering boys. They argued about what music to put on, about which was the quickest way to get there, about who should drive. Zek started off behind the wheel but Connor kept nagging him for a go. Gail put an end to that one by making Zek pull over and driving Agatha herself.

It was a constant whirlwind of punching, pulling and poking. Milly, who hadn't spent much time with boys before, was stunned. How they could be so continually mean, while at the same time it was clear they all loved each other deeply? They insulted each other constantly and just laughed it off. Connor was frequently the butt of their jokes, but she noticed that whenever Tom thought they'd gone too far with Connor he'd get them to ease off and squeeze Connor's cheeks affectionately. Or when Niv got frustrated that he wasn't making himself understood, Zek would focus all of his attention on what his brother was saying. Even if he would then mistranslate it, just for a laugh.

They cracked long-running jokes that Milly didn't understand and rude ones she pretended not to. They burst into song and reminisced about their early gigs. Milly let it all wash over her, the chatter of their voices soothing her weary brain.

Only JD didn't join in. He sat at the back of the bus, wearing large black headphones and staring out at the lake whizzing past the windows. Milly had seen boys like JD before, moodily moving through school corridors and leaving girls sighing in their wake. She'd always assumed it must have been an act, because no one could be that cool all the time. But it seemed that JD could.

She didn't care what all the sighing girls thought, she liked nice boys. Boys who laughed and made her feel like she was someone worth getting to know, not boys who made her feel clumsy and stupid. If this were a TV show, she would most definitely be Team Tom. Almost definitely.

"So, Milly," Tom said, making her jump. She hoped he hadn't noticed the way she'd been looking at JD. "We haven't asked you yet, are you a Slay fan?"

The other boys stopped chattering to turn and look at Milly. She felt embarrassment prickle at her cheeks. "Um…" She didn't need to say any more.

"She hates us!" Tom said, clutching at his chest and falling to the floor as if he'd been struck a mortal blow.

Get off the bus, Niv signed, but he did so with a large smile that let her know he wasn't serious.

"No, it's not that at all, it's just…my mother never let me listen to modern music. And I was only allowed to play classical pieces on the piano. But I like what little I've heard and I'm sure if I heard more I'd…"

"Still hate it?" Zek said, and the other boys chuckled.

"She clearly has good taste then," Milly heard JD say from behind.

Everyone turned to look at JD. He was still staring out of the window, as if he hadn't said anything, but there was a small smile itching at the corner of his mouth. Suddenly, the boys all grabbed whatever was at hand and threw it at him. JD yelped and ducked behind the chair as a sneaker flew over his head. When the assault was over, he came out with his hands up. He smiled at Milly – the first time she'd seen him smile properly – and sat back in his seat, pulling his headphones back on.

Tom clambered into the seat opposite Milly. He leaned in, keeping his voice low. "JD likes to pretend he's too cool for all the pop stuff. But he loves it as much as the rest of us. You might too, if you, you know, gave it a chance." Tom looked down and started drawing a circle on the table between them with his finger. It made a soft squeaking sound.

"I'm sure I will love it," Milly said. And then blushed as she made brief eye contact with Tom.

"Well, if you want to listen to some…" He reached into his pocket and handed over a mobile phone wrapped with a set of white earphones. "It's my spare one and I was thinking, as you left your phone behind… It's got all our songs on it and some other stuff that I love."

"Thanks," Milly said, taking the phone. "I'll listen to them as soon as I get a chance."

"Yes!" Connor shouted from behind them. He'd challenged Zek to an arm wrestle and it looked like he'd won.

"Best of three," Zek said, rubbing his arm.

"Oh, I can keep doing this all day," Connor said, rolling up his sleeves to reveal a tattoo of a five-pointed star – the same tattoo that Tom had, she realized.

"You ever tried reverse arm-wrestling?" Milly asked.

Connor tilted his head to one side and looked at Milly. "You wanna take me on, girlie? Well come on then!" He pushed Tom out of the way and sat down in front of Milly, then spun his baseball hat around to the back and got into position: elbow on the table, muscles tensed. "To make it fair, like, you can use both hands," Connor said.

"How kind." Instead of gripping his hand in the usual way, Milly wrapped her hands over Connor's fist.

"So, in reverse arm-wrestling, you pull towards you, and I pull towards me." Milly heard Zek stifling a laugh behind her. "On three. One, two, three," she said.

Connor pulled away from her and she pulled against his hands with all her strength. She stood up, putting her whole weight into it.

"Cheat all you like, you're going d—" Before Connor could finish, Milly let go and, with a resounding *thwack*, Connor punched himself in the nose.

He blinked in shock; his pale blue eyes watered. Red patches spread across his cheeks and Milly felt suddenly sick at the thought that she might have just given him a pair of black eyes. It was a joke her father had taught her. She hadn't meant to actually hurt him.

"Oh God, I'm so—"

Connor burst out laughing and rubbed at his nose. "Do it on JD!" he said.

JD pulled his headphones off. "Do what on me?" he said.

"What's going on back there?" Gail called.

"Milly's going to teach JD how to reverse arm-wrestle!" Connor said, apparently delighted by this new game.

Gail's sigh carried all the way down the bus. "If you can hold off killing each other for just a few more minutes, we're nearly there."

They drove through the large gates welcoming visitors to the university campus and pulled up in the parking lot. Milly had always imagined university as a place where young people who were hungry for knowledge sat around drinking coffee and arguing over philosophy. But looking out the bus windows, all she saw were students lazing on the grass with books lying ignored by their sides.

"Okay," Gail said, killing the engine. "Milly and Tom, go check out this professor. The rest of us will stay here and dial in for the interview."

"Aw, but…" Connor moaned. He already had his skateboard under his arm.

"But nothing. We owe Jack Caroll; he took us seriously when no one else would."

Connor slumped back into his chair.

"I think it would be better if I stayed here and JD went," Tom said.

"What?" Milly said at the same time as JD. His jaw clenched and he didn't look too impressed at the idea of having to accompany Milly. She wasn't too excited by it either.

"You're always saying you're better at reading people than me," Tom said, with a mischievous smile.

"Well, yeah, but I didn't mean… Besides, what about the interview?"

"Oh, I think we have that taken care of," Zek said.

He nodded at Niv, who pulled up an app on his phone. A few button presses later and JD's voice came out of the speaker. *"Yes. No. I guess. For the music."*

"We took the liberty of sampling a few of your previous answers," Zek said. "Did you know you have said 'For the

music' a total of seventeen times in the last eleven interviews?"
JD glowered at him. "I guess moody looks don't come over
as well on radio. Shame. You've got them down."

"So, you guys go have fun," Tom said.

Milly thought she knew what was going on. Tom was
trying to force her and JD to spend some time together so
they would learn to get along. She didn't think it was going
to work but she didn't want to argue with anyone.

"Come on, let's get it over with." She slumped off the bus
with JD following her.

"Bring us back a doughnut," Connor said as they left.

Run (for my love)

JD pulled his beanie hat down low as he and Milly walked down the wide sidewalk leading to the anthropology department.

JD had always hated school and, as far as he could tell, university looked the same, only bigger. At least school wasn't something he had to worry about now. Gail home-schooled them all – well, bus-schooled them. And without the scowling teachers and teasing kids, he'd found he liked learning. Although a lot of their lessons weren't exactly on subjects that would come up in exams.

He assumed Milly would feel right at home here, but when he looked across at her he wasn't so sure. She looked uneasy too. They really had to find her some new clothes – she was getting stares in Tom's baggy jeans and retro gamer T-shirt.

"Cool tee," one girl said, pointing at the lurid rainbow colours.

"Oh, thanks," Milly replied, looking down at her shirt. "I've never had anyone compliment my outfit before," she said to JD. "Maybe I should let Tom pick all of my clothes in future."

Future, JD thought. Did Milly really have a future with them? At first, he had wanted her out of their lives as quickly as possible, but now he wasn't so sure. The way she'd found out about Big T and Mourdant was impressive and the other boys seemed to like having her around. He didn't want to admit it, but she was growing on him. Not that he'd ever tell her that.

The silence between them was becoming heavy. Milly kept making small noises as if she was about to speak, but then would quickly close her mouth again. It was starting to grate on his nerves.

"You don't have to pretend, you know," he said, to break the tension.

Milly blinked at him, her brow furrowed. "Pretend what?"

"That it's not hurting. I get it, believe me. But it doesn't help."

"Oh, right, thanks," Milly said, her voice sharp with sarcasm. "So I'm supposed to do what exactly? Curl up in a ball and cry?"

JD shrugged. "That's pretty much what I did when my aunt died. And I didn't even like her much."

"And did that help?"

JD stopped walking and considered this for a moment. "Not really. I mean the pain never quite goes away. But you do get used to it. It becomes, I don't know, a part of you, I guess."

"How do you deal with it?" Milly looked up at him, and JD felt her eyes scanning his, as if looking for an answer.

"By punching things." He smiled. For years before Gail found him he'd been getting in trouble for fighting, for being angry all the time. Now, it was his anger that made him so good at what he did.

"Punch therapy. I should have given that a go when my father died."

JD had forgotten about Milly's dad. Here he'd been telling her all about loss, when she was more than familiar with it already.

"What was he like?" he asked.

"The best." Milly looked down at her feet. "Kind, patient, everything my mother wasn't."

"I hardly knew my dad. He was locked up in prison before I was born," JD said, surprising himself. He never spoke about his past, but somehow it seemed natural with Milly. "Mum took me to see him once or twice, but I used to cry so much that she stopped. After she dumped me with her sister, I never heard from either of them again. I got his name and her hair and that was it."

"His name?"

"Joshua Deacon. But I hated him so much I decided to go by JD."

"So that's what it stands for? I wondered."

They walked in silence for a bit longer, before rounding a corner into a large, grass-covered quad. Students lay sunbathing. Others played frisbee. They didn't have a care in the world while he and the rest of Slay fought to keep them safe. Sometimes he wished he could be more like them.

"Oh! My! God!" a girl's voice screamed.

JD winced; he knew what was coming next. The baggy hat hadn't been enough to stop him being recognized. He grabbed Milly's hand. "Run!"

But it was too late. He looked back over his shoulder to see a group of girls chasing after them.

"It's JD! It's JD!"

"Does this happen all the time?" Milly said, struggling to keep up as JD dragged her around a building.

"Pretty much. Quick, in here."

He yanked open a door, pushing Milly inside the small dark room beyond, then slammed it shut behind them. The lock was broken, so he pressed his body against the door, hoping the girls hadn't seen him duck in here. He heard footsteps and people calling out his name.

"Why are we hiding in a toilet, JD?" Milly whispered, her breath warm against his ear.

JD looked down at the cracked tiles under his feet. He was standing in a suspiciously yellow puddle of liquid. "We're hiding from fans," he said, keeping his voice as low as possible.

"You are kidding me?" Milly said, laughing. "You run straight into fights with demons, but you run away from a bunch of your...your fans?" Milly laughed so hard, she could hardly breathe.

JD felt her body shaking against his back. "Shut up," he hissed. "They'll hear us."

"And what? Fan...you to death?"

Milly sounded like Gail. His manager would have told him to get his butt out there and smile. To let them take their selfies and thank them for their support. But he just didn't have the strength for it right now. He twisted around to face Milly. Their bodies were only a handful of centimetres apart. A tear of laughter rolled down her cheekbone.

"It just freaks me out. All these people I've never met, grabbing me and poking me, wanting pictures with me. Sometimes it gets too much."

Milly sucked on her bottom lip, buttoning down the laughter. "I'm sorry, but from the outside it just seems so glamorous."

"Well, it's not."

"Yeah, I see that now," Milly said, giving their less than salubrious surroundings a meaningful look.

JD sighed. "I didn't get into this for the fame or the money or the girls…" As he said that he felt acutely aware of how close he and Milly were. Acutely aware of a lock of her dark hair brushing the tip of her small nose. He looked quickly up at the ceiling. There was a damp patch that looked like a mushroom. "I did it for…"

"For the music?" Milly said.

JD snorted at that. And after a while, both of them were hissing with barely suppressed laughter.

"You're okay, you know?" Milly said when the laughter had passed. "Like, deep, *deep* down." She poked him in the chest three times, indicating where his heart should be. "And I get why you've been such a jerk to me – I wouldn't want me tagging along either."

"It's not that, I promise, it's just…" Milly looked up at him, her large dark eyes shining in the dim light of the toilet. He sighed. "I've been a jerk, you're right. I'm sorry. I'm not good with new people."

"Me neither. I've only really got one friend, and we only became close because we were weirdos together." She shifted away a little, trying to put space between them, but it was difficult with the toilet and sink in the way.

"I never had any friends before Tom and the others," JD said, leaning against the tiled wall and then instantly regretting it when he felt something damp against his skin. "And they only put up with me because we're stuck on a tour bus together. And because Gail makes them."

"Nah, you guys love each other," Milly said. "It's clear. Especially you and Tom."

"Well, Tom's like a brother to me. They all are really."

"It must be nice."

JD thought about the way he and the boys were with each other and realized Milly was right. They were like a family – they'd bicker and fall out, but they never stopped caring for each other. He felt worse than ever about how he'd been treating Milly. She didn't have anyone at all. He promised himself that he was going to work harder at making her feel welcome. Maybe it wouldn't be so terrible if she had to stick around for a little longer.

"I guess I have one more friend now."

He reached out his hand, awkward in the tight space. Milly took it and they shook. Her hand felt cool in his damp one, her eyes looked even bigger in the low light. She really was very pretty, but more than that, she was smart and able to handle herself. The handshake went on for a moment too long and when they finally pulled away JD felt hot and sweaty. It was getting stuffy in here.

He pressed his ear against the door and heard nothing from the other side. "Come on, I think it's safe."

They made it to the anthropology department without any further drama and were directed towards Professor Diaz's office by a grumpy old man wearing a jacket with leather elbow patches.

"Watch yourself though," the man said, his voice muffled by the bushiest beard JD had ever seen. "That one is loco." He further emphasized his opinion by making a corkscrew motion next to his head.

JD hesitated before knocking.

"What are you waiting for?" Milly asked.

"Look, I think you should let me do the talking, okay? There are rules with this kind of thing so…just follow my lead?"

Milly rolled her eyes and knocked before JD could stop her.

"My visiting hours are 10 a.m. till 2 p.m. on Saturday," a heavily accented voice called out from inside.

JD checked his watch. "It's 10.35."

The door flew open. "Is it?"

JD didn't know what he'd been expecting of Professor Diaz. What he certainly had not been expecting was the person who greeted them. She had light brown skin and curly black hair piled up on her head, held precariously in place with a pair of scissors. Propped on top were not one but two pairs of glasses.

"Diaz?" JD said. "Professor Diaz?"

"I wonder," she said, looking up to the sky, "just how old I need to get before people stop looking at me like that?

133

Thirty? Forty? Maybe when I am dead and buried finally they will believe the words carved on my headstone. Yes, I am a professor. Yes, I am young. And yes, I am a woman. Are we done? Good, now come." She gestured them inside.

There was hardly any room for the three of them what with the piles of books, papers and mysterious boxes everywhere. Gail would love it here, JD thought, scanning the leather-bound books on history, religion and mythology. The professor threw herself into a creaking chair and put her feet up on a pile of papers on her desk. She wore a pair of tattered white trainers with tweed trousers and a mismatched waistcoat, under which was a faded grey T-shirt with three red Xs across it. She looked from JD to Milly. The office was hot and stuffy and smelled of damp books and dust.

"Well?"

"We need your help."

"I gathered as much when you knocked on my door. If it's about admissions, you must speak to the dean and if it's about what happened in Belize, well as I told the police it was all a mis—"

"It's about Tezcatlipoca," JD said, pleased with himself for getting the name right.

Diaz pursed her lips. "What do you know about Tezcatlipoca?"

"Not much. That he was an Aztec god," said Milly.

"Not just *a* god," Diaz replied. "Probably *the* god. A god

134

of destruction, the bringer of death, the god of the night sky. Western thinking would label him evil, but the Aztec people understood there is no true good or evil, simply opposing sides in an eternal battle. Worship of Tezcatlipoca died out with the Aztecs."

"Can you tell us anything about this?" JD said, pulling Mourdant's diary out of his back pocket. He handed it over open on the page they had been unable to read.

Diaz squinted at the page, then held it up to the light. "Gah! Where are my glasses?"

Milly pointed. "On your head?"

Diaz patted her hair and pulled the first pair of glasses down into place.

"Not them. My reading glasses!"

"Still on your head," JD said. The old guy had been right, she was a bit unbalanced.

With the correct pair of glasses on, Diaz scanned the writing, and went pale. "This can't be…"

"What is it?"

"It's an obscure Aztec script. Hand me that book behind you. The green one."

JD turned and was faced with a wall of books. More than half of them were green.

"The one on the bottom left."

"This one?" He pulled a huge tome out from the shelf, coughing as it kicked up a cloud of dust.

"Yes, here, here." Diaz pushed papers off her desk to make room for the book. She hefted it open and flicked through stained pages till she found what she was looking for. "Yes, here is the codex I was after."

After about ten minutes of scanning from the diary to the book, and plenty of muttering, she pushed her glasses back up on her head and let out a long whistle.

"What does it say?" JD said.

She said something to herself in Spanish, then looked up at them as though she'd forgotten they were there. "I have read something...similar before, only this is not good."

"So...what does it say?" he asked again.

"Have you ever heard of the Toxcatl Massacre? Why am I even asking? Of course you haven't," Diaz said. "Toxcatl was the Aztec festival in honour of Tezcatlipoca, held at the end of the fifth month. The festivities ended with a sacrifice to the god. Before sunrise, a young man would walk up the steps of the pyramid and surrender his body to the priests. Sacred songs were sung and the man's heart carved out and offered up to the god of darkness. In one of my books, I compare the sacrifice ritual to the Christian Easter. Anyway, on the twenty-second of May 1520, Spaniards had conquered the Aztec capital in Mexico, but the Aztec king, Montezuma, asked permission to celebrate Toxcatl in the usual fashion of his people. Permission was granted. However, after the festivities started the Spaniards interrupted the celebration, killing almost everyone there. Men, women and children alike. Here, let me read you part of the Aztec report." She yanked out a book that had been propping up a table leg, and the table lurched forwards. JD noticed that Diaz's photo was on the back cover of the book.

The professor flicked to a page and began to read. "*The celebration was at its height. Voices were raised in song, hands held in dance. Then, as the sun hit the altar, that was when the Spaniards attacked.*" She closed the book. "It was reported that they even killed the head priestess, Zyanya."

Milly gasped and JD quickly placed his finger to his lips. There was only so much they could give away. But Diaz was so absorbed in her story she didn't seem to notice.

"The chances of this diary coming to me now are…well. Coincidence doesn't cover it."

"What do you mean?" Milly said.

"I have made the study of Aztec rituals my life's work and what you have here," Diaz said, tapping the pages of the diary, "is the first new evidence regarding the Toxcatl ritual in over a decade. Of course, I'd have to authenticate it, consult with some of my colleagues…"

"WHAT DOES IT SAY?" JD said, finally losing his temper.

Diaz looked completely nonplussed that a young man had just shouted at her in her own office. She smiled. "What it *says* is that Zyanya wasn't killed, only terribly wounded.

137

Near death, she escaped with a group of elite Aztec holy warriors called Jaguar Warriors, and travelled to an abandoned temple in the east determined to complete the ritual. Only…"

"Only what?"

"Only she wasn't content with just a sacrifice to appease the god. She wanted revenge. With her dying breath she wanted to bring down the wrath of Tezcatlipoca on all her enemies. The ritual described here isn't a sacrifice," Diaz said, laying her hand over the diary. "It's a summoning. She was going to summon her god."

"So what happened?"

"I don't know. There are pages missing, see? Torn out of the back."

JD looked at some ragged edges left at the back of the diary. He hadn't noticed that earlier.

"We don't know where the person who wrote this account got their information from, but if it's true one can only assume Zyanya's ritual was unsuccessful. Maybe she died before she was able to finish it? Or maybe it was just ghost stories told to scare the conquistadors?"

"Does it say anything about a blade? A blade of shadows?" Milly asked.

JD rolled his eyes. What was Milly doing, giving up that information? He shouldn't have brought her with him. She didn't know the first thing about investigations.

Diaz's eyes tightened. "How do you know about that? What is this? Are you spies from the Field Museum? Get out!" She stood up and jabbed a finger towards the door.

"No, no," JD said, raising his hands in a calming gesture. "We, um, we just…" He racked his brain, trying to think of a way out of the mess Milly had dropped them in.

But before he could, Milly made it even worse. "The priestess Zyanya is back! She's possessed my mother's body and we think she's going to try and bring back Tezcatlipoca and she needs the Blade of Shadows to do it."

JD gasped. He couldn't believe Milly. There were rules. Rules to keep them and civilians safe. And Milly had broken the most important one: keep the existence of demons secret.

Diaz fell back in her chair, stunned. "*Dios mío*," she said.

Nobody said anything for the longest time. JD wanted to run out of there, but he knew he'd have to come up with some excuse. Say the girl was mad. That it had all been a joke. This was what Zek was best at. That boy could talk his way out of any situation. Or Tom, Tom could use his hypnotic skills and make anyone forget anything, even a whip-smart professor like this one. JD was no good at talking people round, but he was going to have to give it a go.

"I think there has been a mis—"

But before he could finish, Diaz cut him off. "Last year, I led an excavation expedition to the Yucatán Peninsula in Mexico. A new Aztec pyramid had been discovered and we were there to uncover and preserve it. After centuries buried under rocks and grass, we were some of the first non- indigenous people to set foot on the site since it was abandoned in the fifteen-hundreds. We don't know what the Aztec people called it, but we named it *Teocalli-Ome*, meaning House of Two Gods, because the symbols of two gods were carved on the walls. Quetzalcoatl, god of light, and Tezcatlipoca, god of darkness. We believe the pyramid was shared by the gods, passing from one to the other with each turn of the calendar wheel – every fifty-two years. On the top level of the pyramid, as well as the remains of humans in what appeared to be ceremonial garb, we found a knife. A black knife, made from obsidian. There have been many obsidian knives uncovered in Aztec burial sites, but this…this was the most beautiful thing I had ever seen. So black that it swallowed light. So perfect that it was hard to imagine it was carved by a human hand. It was etched with symbols I didn't have time to translate. And yes, it is mentioned in this diary. Here." She pointed to a black squiggle on the last page: a jagged, pointed oval with a swirl through the middle. "It says it was used in the ritual, but how must be on the missing pages."

"Do you still have the blade?" JD said, hope bubbling in his stomach.

Could it be this simple? If the ritual couldn't work

without the knife, then all they had to do was keep it safe and stop Mourdant and Zyanya getting it.

"No. Because a team from the Chicago Field Museum swooped in and claimed it. Something to do with them having jurisdiction over Mesoamerican finds in the area. *Tonterías!* Poppycock," she said, standing up and throwing her arms in the air. "They stole it, pure and simple. And those, those…amateurs! They're going to put it on display at their museum tonight."

So close, JD thought, *and yet still so far.*

"Well it's simple," Milly said.

JD looked over at her, confused. She didn't look concerned at all. In fact, there was a glint in her eye that he could have sworn was excitement.

"It is?" Diaz said.

"It is?" JD said, looking at her with a raised eyebrow.

"Yes," Milly said, looking from him to Diaz, as if what she was about to say was obvious. "We go steal it back."

Hot on your trail

"We're Slay and you're listening to 75FM, where the hits keep coming," the four boys chanted in unison as Milly walked through the door of the bus.

"Perfect!" a smooth voice replied over the sound desk speakers. "Thanks, y'all. Great to have you on the show."

"Thanks for having us," JD said quickly, pushing Milly aside so he could get to the mics – a little more roughly than was necessary, she felt. She slid out of the way and took a seat.

"Any time, JD," the voice on the other end of the line said. A soft click signalled the end of the call.

"That was four words!" Zek said. "Positively sparkling."

JD flicked Zek's ear. "Did Jack notice I wasn't here?"

"No," Zek said, rubbing his lobe. "In fact, if anything, I would say it was one of your better interviews."

"Great. Maybe I'll never have to do another one again."

Tom laughed. "Gail might have something to say about that. Although she's currently pretty distracted by screaming at the coconut people. Something about behind-the-scenes pictures not being in our contracts."

Angry shouting and the occasional thud could be heard from Gail's room at the back of the bus. Milly thought about asking who the "coconut people" were and then thought better of it.

"Did you bring me my—" Connor's question was cut off as JD threw a greasy paper bag at him. He pulled out the frosted doughnut, looked at it as if he was in love, then shoved the whole thing into his mouth. "Ank oo," he said, spitting sugar everywhere.

"How did you two get on?" Tom said.

"Um…" Milly looked over at JD. They *had* been getting on, and she'd even felt like they were starting to bond. But since leaving Diaz's office, JD hadn't said a word to her. She got that he had a way of doing things and that maybe she could have kept her mouth shut. She got that Slay were meant to be the experts here. But this was as much her business as theirs. It was *her* mother who had been possessed by an Aztec priestess set on wreaking vengeance on the world, after all. Her gut had told her to trust Professor Diaz and she'd been proved right. They would have never found the location of the Blade of Shadows so quickly otherwise. She wondered if that was what annoyed JD most of all.

Being around JD felt like being on a roller coaster – she never quite knew what was coming next. Maybe that's why he made her feel so jittery all the time, like she couldn't catch her breath?

"Well, Milly blew our cover," JD said.

"What?" Zek said.

"I'm sure she didn't mean to," Tom said, his eyes pleading with her.

"I told the professor about my mother. About the possession," Milly said, irritated by their reactions.

The boys said nothing.

Nevertheless, she persisted. "And it was a good thing I did, because she told us everything we needed to know and now we have a plan."

"*You* have a plan," JD said, spinning a chair around and sitting on it backwards. He was the only person Milly had ever seen do that who didn't look like he was trying too hard. "*I* didn't agree to anything."

Milly looked pleadingly at Tom. She would need their help.

Tom softened and sat down opposite her. "Tell us what happened."

Milly relayed everything as quickly and as simply as she could. What Professor Diaz had said about Tezcatlipoca and the massacre. And about how she had translated the diary. "It's a ritual to summon Tezcatlipoca. And Zyanya is back to finish what she started."

144

Milly enjoyed the look of shock on the boys' faces. It was nice to be the one delivering the news for once, rather than just being on the end of it.

"A ritual to summon a god?" Connor said, his mouth still full of doughnut.

"Summon a goat?" Zek said. "Well, that is new."

"God!" Connor said, spraying everyone with crumbs.

Zek let out a disgusted squeal and dusted the crumbs off his white T-shirt. "I thought you said it was a ritual to honour Big T, not one to actually bring him back."

"We were wrong," JD said.

"A ritual to summon the god of death and shadows from the Netherworld?" Tom swallowed hard, his Adam's apple bobbing beneath his buttoned-up shirt.

"Yes," JD said.

Wow. That's big, signed Niv.

Connor threw himself down next to Milly, the force of his bounce nearly throwing her off the sofa. "So we stop it from happening. Simple."

"Oh, sure, easy," Zek said, shaking his head at Connor.

"Go on," JD said. "Tell them the rest."

"The Blade of Shadows – the one we know Mourdant and Zyanya are after, the one that Diaz says was used in the failed summoning ritual back in 1520 – it's going on display at the Field Museum tonight."

"Brilliant. Amazing work." Tom sat on the other side of

Milly. While JD made her feel unsettled, Tom's presence was soothing, calm. She felt that as long as he was next to her, everything would find a way of working itself out.

Niv pointed to the floor. *Here?*

"Yes, in Chicago."

"Well, how about that for a coincidence?" Zek said. "The blade just so happens to be brought to the same city that Mourdant is in."

"We should be careful. The blade could be a cursed object, like the Lydian Hoard, the Argonaut treasure, Tutankhamun's tomb. Anyone who came into contact with them met with a nasty fate."

Everyone stared at Connor, surprised and impressed.

"What? I read as much as you lot."

Cereal packets, Niv signed.

"What did he say? Milly, tell me what he said."

Milly hid her smile and decided to protect Connor from this one. "You really should learn sign, Connor."

Niv crossed his arms and smiled smugly.

"She hasn't finished yet," JD said, leaning his chin on the back of the chair.

The boys turned back to Milly. It had all seemed so simple back in Diaz's office. So clear. But now, under the intense stare of the five boys, she wasn't so sure. "Well—"

"She thinks we should steal it," JD finished.

There was another silence among the boys, this one

punctuated by more shouting coming from the back of the bus.

"Well, damn, Milly," Zek said finally. "I like your style."

Milly smiled.

"Yeah, if we get the blade first then they can't complete the ritual. No ritual, no end of the world. I like it." Connor held up a hand for Milly to high-five and she responded.

JD straightened up. "Are you kidding me?" he said. "This is a dumb plan."

"Do you have a better one?" Tom said.

JD opened his mouth and closed it again. "Well, no. But…"

"But nothing. The priority has to be stopping Mourdant and Zyanya getting the blade, don't you think?"

"I guess."

Milly wanted to rewind to an hour before, when she and JD had been hiding together, when they had shaken hands and she'd felt like they might actually become friends. "JD," she said, "we won't do this unless you think it's the right thing to do."

They all waited to see what JD would say.

"Call up the security on the museum," JD said, standing up. "Let's see how hard it's going to be to break in."

Connor leaped up. "Ooooh, we could do the old Mission Impossible. Hang from a rope and that."

I could hack the CCTV, Niv signed.

147

"Or," Milly said, "we could just walk through the front door? They're having a launch party tonight."

"Won't it be invites-only?"

Milly couldn't believe what she was hearing. "Um, don't you guys know who you are?"

The boys looked from one to another.

Milly took pity on them. "You're the world's number one boy band. I think you can probably swing some invitations to a party at a museum."

Zek laughed. "I like her. Have I said how much I like her?"

"You might have mentioned it," JD said, a small smile twitching at the corner of his mouth.

"Will there be food?" Connor asked.

"One small thing." Milly looked down at her borrowed clothes. She had a wardrobe full of awful dresses her mother had made her wear to various opening nights, but they were all back at the house. "I don't have anything to wear."

Party like it's our last

The museum looked more like an ancient temple than anything. Long white steps led up to slender columns, on which perched a triangular pediment covered in carvings. Between the columns hung large red banners advertising the new exhibit: *Wonders of the Aztec World*. Men in handmade suits and tuxedos and women in tight-fitting cocktail dresses and gaudy ballgowns made their way up the steps and disappeared inside.

"Ready?" Tom said.

JD sighed. "Can't we just break in after everyone has gone home?"

Zek straightened his jacket. "Well, I look incredible in this suit, so I'm not climbing around in any air ducts tonight."

"We all look pretty hot, if you ask me," Connor said.

"Did you have to wear the baseball cap?"

"It's my thing."

"Your thing?" Zek said.

"Sure. Tom has his ugly jumpers…"

"Oi!"

"Niv has his hipster buttoned-up shirts, JD rocks that fifties rebel thing and you, well you wear women's V-necks."

Zek looked down at the black T-shirt he wore under his suit. It was cut low enough to show off the curve of his pectoral muscles. "Fair."

"Speaking of looking incredible…"

JD looked to see what was causing Tom's jaw to hang loose. It was Milly.

When Gail heard their plan she, like the others, had said that Milly had done a great job and then insisted they must all look the part. "This is a public appearance and an opportunity to build your brand."

The boys all had suits for such occasions, but Milly only had what Tom had lent her. So Gail had whisked Milly off on a shopping spree. The results of which were now sweeping across the plaza towards them.

Milly wore a long red dress that brushed the ground. She'd had her hair done too. Rather than her usual blunt bob, her hair was swept back and pinned with glittering grips. She looked beautiful, JD thought, but uncomfortable.

Tom was just gawping. "Milly, you look—"

"Like an idiot, I know. I can hardly walk in these heels. But Gail is really persuasive."

"'Idiot' wasn't *quite* the word I was going for," Tom said with a cough.

JD noticed how red his cheeks were.

"Where *is* Gail?" Zek asked.

"About an hour ago she said something about coconuts again and started shouting at someone on the phone. When the car turned up at the store she was still shouting and told me to go ahead."

"Ah, I love our manager," Zek said.

Tom crooked his elbow towards Milly. "Shall we?"

Milly laughed and took Tom's arm. The two of them walked up the steps together. JD watched his friend with Milly and something heavy sank into his stomach. He knew Tom liked her, that much was clear, but in that moment JD realized just how much. And what made him feel even weirder was how much Milly clearly liked Tom in return. She laughed at his jokes, stared deep into his eyes. Watching them, JD felt like he was stuck on the outside. He liked Milly – she was super-smart and funny and he felt like he could talk to her in a way he'd never been able to talk to a girl before. He'd even got over how she had ignored him and taken the lead back with Diaz. But that didn't mean that he *liked* her liked her. Did it?

Niv appeared by his shoulder and gave him a sympathetic look. He pointed to JD then made the "okay" symbol while raising his eyebrows in a question.

"Sure, why wouldn't I be?" JD said.

Niv pointed at Milly. She tucked a curl of hair behind her ear nervously and laughed at yet another of Tom's jokes.

"What about her?"

Niv rested both hands on his chest above his heart.

"Don't be stupid," JD said. "Of course I don't. What would make you... I mean, no. Of course not. Stupid."

Niv raised his hands in mock surrender and shrugged.

"Just shut up, okay?"

Niv shook his head, hiding a smile, and JD walked quickly away. Niv was too observant for his own good sometimes.

JD headed up the stairs. At the top, a woman wearing a low-cut black dress and holding a clipboard smiled without her eyes. "Invitations, please."

"Our names are on the list," Tom said. "It's Slay and..." He looked down at Milly. "And friend."

The woman's eyes widened. "Oh my, well, yes. You must go in. Have a wonderful evening and if you need anything, anything at all, you know where I am."

JD shuddered as she laid a long-taloned hand on his arm. "Thanks," he said, walking by.

Through the arched black doors, they were greeted by the huge skeleton of a dinosaur with its jaws wide open. It looked ready to eat everyone at the party.

"Boys, spread out," JD said under his breath. "Milly, stay close to me."

Tom hesitated for a moment before letting go of Milly's arm and heading for one side of the room. JD hadn't meant to split them up like that, he'd just been following standard procedure. He was almost totally certain he hadn't anyway.

String music floated up to the high ceiling, mixing with the chatter and laughter of the champagne-swilling guests. JD was never going to get used to evenings like these. Everyone looked so at ease, so pleased with themselves.

"God, I hate these places. These people," Milly said, echoing JD's thoughts.

"Do you know them?"

"I know their type. The same set would come to my mother's opening nights and tell her how simply marvellous she was, while being awful behind her back. They think just because they're rich it makes them better than everyone else."

"Aren't you rich?"

Milly seemed to bristle at his question and JD instantly regretted it.

"Aren't you?" she snapped back.

"Yeah, but…" He wanted to say that it was different when you're born poor. That no amount of zeroes in your bank account would ever make you feel like you belonged in a place like this. But he didn't.

"Feeding your burning intellectual curiosity, I see?"

JD turned to see a woman wearing a sharp three-piece

suit with pointed black heels. It took him a while to recognize her, as she looked older than she had in her office. "Professor Diaz?"

"Did you already forget that we agreed to meet here? You are going to have to work on your memory skills." She turned to Milly. "Aren't these things awful?"

"The worst," Milly agreed.

A waiter shoved a silver tray filled with tiny indistinguishable pastry parcels under JD's nose. He took one just to make the man go away.

Diaz tapped her lip while trying to choose, then took one of each. "I only come for the food. And because laughing at old men's terrible jokes helps with funding."

JD choked on his canapé. Diaz plucked a glass of champagne off a passing tray and downed it in three smooth gulps, before swapping it for a fresh glass.

"Well, come on then. The blade we're all here to see is over there." She pointed to the middle of the room, where a spotlight picked out a glass cabinet. A large man in a black suit stood beside it, his arms folded. As they got closer, they saw it. A single black knife with a jagged edge, resting on a clear plastic plinth. The blade was carved out of what looked like black glass, while the handle was made of a white material, stone or ivory maybe, and covered in carvings of intricate symbols that looked familiar to JD from the diary. It was undeniably beautiful, a work of exceptional craftsmanship. The blade seemed to soak up the light surrounding it, as if he was looking at a black hole.

"Isn't she beautiful?" Diaz said, with a soft sigh.

"It really is," Milly replied, raising her hand to rest on the glass case of the display cabinet.

"Don't touch!" the man in black barked.

Milly lifted her hand slowly and backed away. *If they couldn't so much as touch the glass, how were they going to get that thing out of here?* JD wondered.

"So," Diaz said, turning away so the security guard couldn't hear her, "what's the plan?"

Milly looked at JD and smiled. "Just follow my lead."

Want to get close to you

"That doesn't look right, does it, professor?" Milly said loudly.

Diaz looked at her, her nose wrinkled above the bridge of her glasses.

"That symbol," Milly continued, hoping that Diaz would catch on. "Isn't that Mayan?"

Diaz looked back at the blade and then comprehension dawned. "Oh, yes, why yes, I think you're right. Yes, that's absolutely not Aztec script. Which can only mean one thing…"

"Diaz," a weary voice said from behind them. "I don't remember inviting you."

Milly turned with Diaz to see a red-faced man in a crumpled suit and bow tie. He held a nearly empty glass of red wine in stubby fingers and his pained smile revealed wine-stained teeth.

"Charles," Diaz said with clear distaste. "I don't remember inviting you to Mexico where you contaminated my dig with your massive shoes and tiny hands and stole MY find!"

"Still bitter I see. Shame, you really should learn to get over things. Can I help it if the Field Museum has richer and better connected patrons than the university? If you are looking for a new position, maybe I can introduce you to my patron? He's coming tonight. I could always do with some more good researchers on my staff."

"I'm not going anywhere near your staff," Diaz said.

The man called Charles chuckled and threw back the last dregs of his wine.

"So how are you going to explain to your patron that that knife is a fake?" Milly said. She liked this man as much as Diaz seemed to.

"A what?" Charles said.

"A fake, Charles," Diaz said. "Do you need your ears testing along with your brain? The carving on the handle isn't Aztec. In fact, I would go as far as to say that what you might be looking at here is a modern replica, tat made to sell to foolish tourists."

"But…but…" Charles spluttered, patches of red appearing on his vein-mottled cheeks. "You were the one who found it."

"And if you remember, I had yet to authenticate it before you and your team stormed in."

"Diaz, I swear, if you have set me up—"

Diaz chuckled, delighted. "Listen, let me offer you a deal – which is more than you offered me. Give me fifteen minutes to examine the blade and if it's fake, as I believe it is, I will say nothing. We'll simply pretend it was never here and no one, not your patron or any of these lovely guests will ever know. But if it's genuine, I want shared credit on the find."

"Hmmm," Charles said, his beady eyes narrowing. "I don't trust you as far as I could throw a tepoztopilli."

"Oh, Charles, Charles! The Aztec didn't throw their tepoztopilli, they were used for hand-to-hand combat, I would have thought you'd know that. But I swear to you, on my name as an archaeologist, I will be one hundred per cent honest with you. You know that much about me."

Charles seemed to consider this. He checked his watch, then glanced at the large doors. "Okay. You have your fifteen minutes and then I want the blade back in its case. She can come. He stays." Then he waved at the security guard. "Unlock it."

Milly looked desperately at JD. She couldn't handle this on her own. But he shook his head the smallest of fractions.

"Okay, I'll wait here, like a good little boy," he said, and Milly knew he had absolutely no intention of staying put. She smiled.

The guard looked confused, his already pug-like face crumpling in on itself with the effort of thought.

"Well? I said unlock it," Charles repeated. "We need to take the blade to be examined."

The security guard unlocked the case while Charles pulled a pair of white gloves out of his back pocket and put them on. Milly watched hungrily as he lifted the blade out of its case.

He carried the blade through the crowd, holding it in front of him as if it was a grenade that might go off any minute. Which in some ways, Milly thought, it was.

"Where are we going?" Milly whispered to Diaz.

"The basement, I'm guessing. He'll want to keep this as contained as possible. Which probably won't make things easy for your friends who are following us." She nodded over her shoulder at Tom, Connor and the twins, who were following at a distance. JD too had slipped away from the guard and was sticking close to them. Diaz had keen eyes. You'd have to look carefully to spot that the boys were on their tail. At first glance, they were five famous boys, surprisingly interested in the exhibits, but there was a certain sense of purpose in their meanderings. They weren't going to let the blade, or Milly, out of their sight.

They followed Charles and the blade through the main hall, weaving through laughing guests and waiters, passing glass cabinets filled with taxidermy seabirds posed mid-flight or perched in trees and, in one case, about to eat a frog. Milly shivered as the glass eyes of the birds seemed to follow her, ready to snap her up in their pincer beaks just like that rubbery frog. Even when they'd left the natural world exhibits behind, she still felt like she was being watched.

They arrived at an elevator marked *Restricted*, with a key-card lock under the call button.

"In my inside pocket," Charles said.

Diaz sighed and reached inside the man's jacket, her face turned away in disgust. She pulled a card pass out with two fingers and pressed it against a panel on the wall. The doors pinged and slid open. Milly followed Diaz and Charles inside. She saw JD and the others only a matter of metres away. But without the key card, how were they going to follow? Milly's mind raced and her hand started to itch in panic. She needed a plan and fast – the elevator doors were already closing.

Diaz was one step ahead of her. When the doors were only a centimetre or so apart, Diaz bent down to adjust her shoe and Milly saw her flick the card out through the gap. Milly gazed at Diaz in dumb adoration. She was the kind of smart Milly always wanted to be. Diaz winked at her as the lift began to move.

There was plenty of room for the three of them and yet Milly still felt a creeping claustrophobia as the lift rumbled downward. Charles muttered under his breath, something about patrons and reputation. Diaz hummed to herself; she seemed to be enjoying all of this. The lift juddered to a halt and they stepped out into darkness.

"Don't move. You will only break something."

Charles vanished into the blackness; only the sound of his shoes could be heard. A moment later, there was a loud clunk of a switch and strip lights blinked on. They were standing in a huge warehouse, filled with crates and exhibits under repair or out of date. It seemed to stretch on and on and on.

"Come. Do not touch anything."

Milly had no intention of touching anything. The stuffed animals and mannequins peeking out of boxes gave her the creeps.

"In there." Charles stopped at a metal door.

Diaz opened the door and stepped back for Charles to go in first with the blade. Milly followed.

The room was painted bright white, with a long metal table lining one wall. A two-metre tall wooden crate marked *Egyptian Exhibit* was propped upright against the wall on the left, while a plaster figure of a caveman holding a club stood on the right.

"Okay then," Charles said, placing the blade on the metal table. "Do your thing." He pulled off his gloves and handed them to Diaz.

"Please," she said, pulling a pair of blue rubber gloves out of her handbag.

She picked the blade up and turned it slowly around in her hands. "It's beautiful," she said. "Truly beautiful."

"I know that," Charles said. "But is it real?"

Diaz shook her head. She, like Milly, had been so lost in staring at the blade that she seemed to have forgotten the whole pretence for why they were here. "It's...I'd like to take it back to my lab."

Charles laughed. "Nice try, Diaz. This blade is not going out of my sight. Now hurry up. You have ten minutes left."

Milly glanced at the door. Where were the boys? If they didn't turn up soon then she was going to have to handle this. She looked around the room for something she could use as a weapon. Her eyes fell on the caveman's club, but as much as she disliked Charles, she didn't think she had it in her to hurt him.

"Hurry up," she muttered.

"What's that?" Charles said. Then he stepped back. "Oh, I see."

"You do?" Diaz asked.

"Yes, you are trying to ruin my night! Fake, my foot. You just said that to try and embarrass me in front of Mourdant."

"Mourdant?" Milly gasped.

"Yes, my patron. He funded the trip to Mexico and he will be arriving any minute to see the blade."

Mourdant was coming. And that probably meant that Zyanya would be too.

Milly stared at Diaz. "Mourdant knew my mother," she said desperately, hoping Diaz would catch on.

"Oh?" Diaz said, her brow furrowed. And then, as realization dawned, "Oh!"

"Right, I've had enough of this. I'm calling security."

"You're doing no such thing, Charles," Diaz said. "You're going to walk out of here and go back to your party, or – and I didn't want to have to do this – or else I am going to tell everyone about what really happened in Belize City."

His eyes went wide and his skin turned a very nasty shade of grey. "You wouldn't."

"Oh, wouldn't I?"

He sputtered, looking from Diaz to the blade.

"I kept your name out of it till now. So the question you have to ask yourself, Charles," Diaz said, "is what's more important to you: this blade or your reputation?"

Charles took all of ten seconds to make his mind up. He adjusted his tie and left the room.

Now, with Charles out of the way, they had to get the blade out of here without Mourdant stopping them. But how?

"There," Diaz said, pointing up at an air duct.

"It's too small for you. Give me the blade."

Diaz pulled off her jacket, wrapped it around the blade, and handed it to Milly. "Please keep it safe."

Milly looked up at the cover of the air duct. The ceiling was high – there was no way she was reaching it alone. "The box," Milly said, pointing at the tall crate in the corner. If they could drag it over, she could clamber up on it.

Diaz helped Milly drag the box underneath the vent and then steadied it. Milly scrambled up, catching the hem of her dress on a nail as she did so. She tugged at it, leaving a swathe of red cloth behind. "Oh well, guess I won't be returning it then."

Holding the bundled-up blade in one hand, she reached up with her other and pushed at the air-vent cover. Mercifully it gave way. She kneeled up on the box, then stood. It swayed beneath her. She reached up, throwing herself forward as the crate went tumbling to the floor, grabbing the edge of the vent and dragging herself inside. She pulled the cover closed behind her, just as she heard the door slam open.

Don't make me fight for our love

JD could have kissed Diaz when he saw the key card come flying out of the gap between the elevator doors.

He stopped it under his foot and checked to see if anyone else had seen. But the party guests were too busy with the free champagne to take any notice.

The other boys drifted towards him, gathering around the elevator.

"Where's she gone?" Tom said, an unfamiliar panic in his voice.

"It's okay," JD said, swooping down to retrieve the key card. He pressed it against the reader and pushed the call button. "We're right behind."

It seemed like a painful wait for the elevator. The laughter from the party was too loud, the music too screechy. They were only lucky that this kind of crowd were less likely to know who they were, so they were mostly ignored. JD did see a young woman staring at him, tugging at the jacket of a man next to her. He turned quickly away, and that was when he saw the man in the sunglasses.

"Oh no."

"What?" Tom said, looking to where JD was staring. "Oh. Mourdant."

Mourdant was drifting through the crowd, grinning widely. He stopped every now and then to kiss some of the guests on both cheeks. Behind him, looking angry and impatient, was Zyanya. She wore a long golden dress that trailed behind her and her hair was piled on her head in intricate plaits. Following them was a very large man wearing a black suit that looked considerably more expensive than the one worn by the museum security guard. They were heading for the cabinet. The empty cabinet.

JD calculated the distance between the demons and the display. Less than a minute and they'd realize the blade was missing and then...

He punched the call button again.

"Come on," Tom said.

"I'm doing it," JD said.

Connor pushed the button a few more times.

"Yeah," JD said, "because I don't know how to push a button."

But at that moment the elevator doors pinged and opened, revealing a very red-faced Charles, who rushed out.

"B...B..." He looked as if he was struggling to speak. "Security?" he finished weakly.

JD grabbed him by his tie and pulled him out of the elevator, before piling in with the rest of the boys. He stared out at the party, his eyes not leaving Mourdant, who had just arrived at the empty glass cabinet. As the doors started to close, the demon looked in his direction and pointed.

"Stop them!"

But Mourdant was too late. The doors had closed and the elevator was already moving.

When they arrived at the basement level, the boys raced out.

"There!" JD said, heading towards a door that was partially open.

He kicked the door fully open and scanned the room. Diaz stood beside the statue of a caveman; on the floor was a broken wooden crate and lying next to it was what looked like a mummy.

"Where's Milly?" Tom said, closing the door behind him.

Diaz pointed up.

JD saw the scrap of red material caught on a nail of the broken box and then followed Diaz's finger. An air vent.

"She's brilliant!" he said, working out what must have happened. "Brilliant."

She had escaped with the Blade of Shadows. So now they

just needed to keep Mourdant and Zyanya from following. The demons couldn't be far behind. Within moments they heard the ping of the elevator arriving.

Diaz reached into her handbag and pulled out a golden lipstick. This was hardly the time for a touch-up, JD thought. But Diaz wasn't reapplying her make-up. She reached into her bag again and pulled out a heavy green book – the one she had been checking in her office. Then she strode over to one of the walls and, consulting the book, started drawing a large circle using the red lipstick.

"Hold them off!" she shouted.

"Ready?" JD said.

"Born ready," the boys replied in unison.

JD pulled out a knife he'd concealed inside the lining of his jacket. The boys did the same, arming themselves with the weapons they'd snuck into the museum and spreading out to make sure they wouldn't get in each other's way. Connor cracked his neck, Zek pulled a collapsible bow staff from his trouser leg and extended it with a flick, Tom loaded his fingers with throwing knives, while Niv stood, a knife held loosely in his hand, head tilted slightly, listening.

"I know you're in there," Zyanya's sing-song voice called out from the other side of the door, as if they were all playing a child's game.

"Yeah, well we know you're out there!" Connor said, his enthusiasm making up for the lack of sense.

"Just give us the blade and no harm will come to you." This was Mourdant.

"Well, maybe a little harm." Zyanya laughed a cold, cruel laugh.

JD looked up at the air vent. He heard scrabbling from above. Whatever happened, he couldn't let them get to the blade. Or to Milly. He'd die before anyone touched her.

"I'd like to see you try," he said.

"Oh, please," Mourdant said. "I beat you easily before. Go on then, priestess. I know you've been dying to let one of your pets out."

Pets? JD wondered. He didn't like the sound of that.

He heard a creaking through the ceiling tiles. They had to cover Milly's escape.

"Come and get it," JD said – and regretted it almost instantly.

There was a sound like fabric tearing followed by a frantic snarling as a creature burst through the door and into the room. Instead of skin, it was covered in slick, bronze fur with black spots. Golden eyes glowed in a head which had maybe once belonged to a man but was now misshapen, with an extended nose and impossibly wide mouth bristling with needle-sharp teeth. It still wore a black suit, but unnatural muscles strained the material to ripping point. Its hands – no, JD corrected himself, its paws – ended in razor-sharp claws and it snarled like the beast it so clearly was.

JD had never seen anything like this in his life. Demons usually tried to pass as human, but this thing had given up any pretence. The creature whipped its head back and forth, looking from boy to boy.

Connor, always the first into the fray, charged, but the creature merely batted him away, sending him flying across the room.

The twins moved, but their way was suddenly blocked as the mummy that had been lying on the floor rose up to its rotten, bandaged feet. Gnarled hands uncurled, reaching for the twins. JD glanced to the door, where he saw a grinning Mourdant with his arms also raised. Somehow, impossibly, the demon was controlling the mummy.

A withered hand wrapped itself around Zek's neck. Niv stabbed the mummy once, then twice, but his attack had zero effect. The corpse grabbed Niv with its other hand and lifted both boys off their feet.

JD was cornered by the beast. He jabbed out with his knife, but the thing dodged his blow and then sideswiped him, knocking his blade out of his hand and him to the floor. His head cracked against the concrete floor and he saw stars. Reacting on instinct, he rolled as the beast pounced, dodging deadly claws just in time. Confused, the beast turned on the caveman statue instead, tearing at its head with powerful jaws. When it realized it was chewing on nothing but plaster and sawdust, it turned back to JD, growling.

JD backed up until he was against the wall. There was nowhere for him to go. Connor lay on the floor, moaning; the twins were still in the grip of the mummy. Only Tom was okay and he was standing in front of Diaz, throwing knives at the ready. Diaz continued to work with her lipstick on the wall, drawing some kind of pattern.

The demon beast came closer and closer. It roared hot stinking breath into his face and foul saliva splattered onto his skin. JD frantically looked for something, anything, to defend himself with and he saw it by his feet. The caveman's club.

It was heavier than he had expected, carved from stone rather than wood. Just as the beast pounced again, he shoved the club hard into its mouth. Powerful teeth slammed down, cracking the stone but not breaking it. The beast snarled, the sound muffled by the club, and shook its head, trying to break free.

JD spun away, readying himself for another attack. His knife lay on the floor. He leaped for it, but was dragged back by four razor-sharp claws digging into the flesh of his leg. He twisted to see the beast bearing down on him, its now empty mouth open in what JD was almost certain was a smile. It came closer and closer, hissing and snarling.

JD stared into the blackness of its maw and wondered if this would be the last thing he ever saw.

Strike back

Milly crawled in darkness, the sound of her thumping heart almost drowning out the shouts and snarls below. Slay had arrived but followed by...what? The noises coming through the duct didn't sound human. She didn't know where she was going, only that she had to keep the blade safe, because if the demons got their hands on it, they'd summon Tezcatlipoca and everything would be lost. She clutched the bundle to her chest, feeling the sharp angles of the blade wrapped inside, and crawled on.

The duct came to a junction. Should she go left or right? Before she could decide, she heard the sound of laughter echoing up the vent from the room behind her. Familiar and yet wrong. Zyanya. The demon priestess was close. Milly froze. Maybe this was her chance for revenge? Zyanya was here, walking around in her dead mother's body, and Milly was holding a weapon.

In the dark, she peeled away the cloth and wrapped her fingers around the hilt of the blade. It fitted perfectly into her grasp, like it had been made for her. A sense of strength seemed to flow through her hand and into her chest. Yes, she could do this. She wasn't going to run away. She was going to take the fight to Zyanya and damn Mourdant or any other demon who tried to stand in her way. Slay had saved her before. Well, now it was time she saved them.

She twisted around in the duct, her skin scraping against metal rivets, and started to crawl back towards the opening, back towards the room. The blade glinted in the dim light spilling into the air vent, almost as if it was sucking in the light. She was close now. The noises coming from beneath her were terrible, snarling, renting, screaming, and yet she wasn't afraid. Maybe for the first time in her life, she wasn't afraid. She was filled with a burning rage and purpose. Kill Zyanya. Get revenge for her mother. Save the boys.

She pushed herself through the opening and crashed to the floor. The room was a whirl of chaos. Connor, crumpled in a heap, not moving; the twins being held aloft by a thing with rotting, peeling flesh, and there, in the doorway, was Mourdant, smiling gleefully, still wearing his sunglasses, his hands curled as if choking the air. Behind him stood Zyanya.

The demon priestess saw Milly and smiled a twisted smile. She wore an expression of glowing pride, which Milly had never, in her whole life, seen on her mother's face. Never, despite every exam passed, award won or lesson learned, had her mother looked so happy with her. She wanted to believe so much that her mother was still in there.

"*Maman?*" Milly said.

"My child." The woman reached out her arms.

She looked at the woman, a moment of hope swelling in her heart. And then the demon's eyes flashed black.

"You're not my mother!" Milly spat. She tightened her grip on the blade and took a step towards the demon priestess. This would end here and now.

Zyanya waved her hand, as if welcoming Milly forward. *Yes*, the demon seemed to say, *come to me, come.*

Milly heard a terrible snarl and saw a hairy thing fly past her, landing on one of the boys. She couldn't see who was being attacked. She looked from Zyanya to the demon beast. It was biting and clawing at whichever boy it had trapped. Milly hesitated for barely a fraction of a second and then turned away from Zyanya and charged at the demon beast. She punched out her hand and stabbed its back with the Blade of Shadows. The blade sliced into the thing's flesh too easily as she stabbed again and again. After a shuddering howl, the beast went still.

"No!" Zyanya cried out and tried to run into the room. With a blood-chilling screech, she was thrown backwards, as if she'd collided with an invisible wall. Through the doorway, Milly saw what had been her mother's body lying on the floor, arms bent at unnatural angles, like a wooden puppet that had had its strings cut.

"Ha! *¡No entrad!*" Diaz cried out.

Milly turned to see the professor standing in front of a symbol drawn in blood-red lipstick. It glowed bright gold.

"Clever," Mourdant said. "But your protection symbol won't last for ever."

"It doesn't need to last for ever." Tom flicked his wrist and a silver shard cut in front of Milly's face, causing a curl of her hair to drift, detached, in the slipstream. She followed the trail as it sliced through the air and punched right through the lens of Mourdant's sunglasses.

The man raised a hand and delicately pulled his shattered sunglasses off, leaving the throwing knife still sticking out of one black eyeball. He looked down at the glasses with his remaining good eye, then back at Tom.

"Oh, no," the demon said, with a sigh.

Tom pulled another blade out of his jacket and drew back his hand, ready to take another shot. He didn't need it. Milly stared, transfixed, as Mourdant started to shiver and shake like he was having a fit. His body started to change, his youthful face creasing into saggy wrinkles, his slicked-back hair turning white and then falling out in chunks, his too-white teeth turning brown and dropping out one by one, clattering to the floor. With a screeching hiss, a black shadow burst out of the withered husk of a body and dissipated, leaving only a swirl of dust.

Milly looked around, trying to process what she was seeing. There was no sign of Zyanya's broken body through the doorway now. Had she too turned to dust? Next to Milly, the thing that had been holding the twins collapsed to the floor, just a pile of bones and rags. Zek and Niv fell to their knees, choking and gasping for breath. Connor groaned and rolled into a sitting position as Tom rushed to help him. That only left JD.

He was still pinned by the body of the beast, his face splattered with blood, and there were deep cuts in his leg. With a kick, Milly rolled the creature over, freeing JD. He stared up at her like he couldn't believe what he was seeing. The others were looking at her too, a mixture of surprise and amusement on their faces.

"Milly?" JD said, like he couldn't believe that the girl who'd saved him and the one standing here now were the same person. It was kind of insulting.

"Well," she said. "Are you going to lie there all day?"

Slip away

The light from Diaz's symbol still glowed.

"What *is* that?" JD asked, wiping the blood from his face.

"Scarlet Heart," Diaz said, reading off the bottom of her lipstick.

"I think he meant—" Tom started.

"I know what he meant," she said, shaking her head. "It's the symbol of Quetzalcoatl. Tezcatlipoca's eternal opposite. God of creation and light."

"And it acts as protection against Tezcatlipoca?" Connor said, walking up to it and tracing his finger around the outline. "That is seriously deadly."

"Seems so." Diaz popped her lipstick and the green book back in her bag.

"Seems? You mean, you didn't know?" JD asked.

"It was an educated guess. Exceedingly educated, if I'm telling the truth. It worked, didn't it? Zyanya couldn't enter the room, which is why she had to send her pet in." Diaz kicked at the body on the floor.

JD turned his attention to the dead demon beast. As he watched, golden fur receded into dark skin, long claws retracted under human fingernails, till the beast had transformed back into the body of a large man, head shaved, empty eyes staring up at the ceiling.

"Oh no," Milly said. "Not him."

"Who?"

"He was my mother's driver," Milly said, covering her mouth with her hand. "He was nice. He liked milkshakes."

JD noticed a rough symbol carved into the man's arm. Had he been a willing host? he wondered. Or had he been forced to give up his body to the demon?

"Didn't the diary say that when Zyanya escaped the massacre she was guarded by a group of Jaguar Warriors?" Zek said. "It seems like at least one has returned to protect her again."

Diaz stood over the body. "I never realized how literal the name Jaguar Warrior was – that they had the power to actually *transform* into jaguars. Fascinating."

"This is a man we're talking about," Milly said, pointing the black blade at the body. "A man that I..."

"You saved me," JD said, before the girl could finish. He could still feel the hot breath of the beast on his face. He had been absolutely sure that he was going to die...and the really worrying thing was that he'd been okay with it. It was how he expected to go out. Screaming into the face of some evil thing. But thanks to Milly, he was still here. Still fighting.

"But you shouldn't have," he finished.

Milly shook her head. "What? You're telling me I should have let you die?"

"I'm telling you," JD said, stepping closer, "that keeping the Blade of Shadows safe is more important than me. More important than any of us." He waved his arm in the direction of the rest of the band.

"The air duct was smart," Tom said, stepping between them.

"Yes, and she should have stayed up there," JD snapped.

"I'll remember that for next time a great big beast is tearing your face off, shall I?"

"Yes!"

JD and Milly glared at each other. JD wanted to thank her; he wanted to wrap her in a hug and make sure she was okay; he wanted to say what he really meant, which was that *she* was the thing that was more important than him or any of them. That it was *her*, not the blade, that he had to keep safe.

"Shame about the dress," Zek said, breaking the tense silence.

"Huh?" Milly looked down at herself and the black grime

that covered the red silk. She then looked at her hand holding the blade. It was coated in the demon beast's blood.

She stretched the blade out in front of her, as if trying to get as far away from it as possible. "Take it, take it," she said to Diaz.

The professor took the blade gently out of Milly's hand, which was shaking along with her whole body. It looked like she might be going into shock. Before JD could move, Tom was there. He rested his hand on Milly's face for a moment, then pulled Milly into a hug. JD felt a sting of envy as the hug went on for an uncomfortably long time.

To distract himself, JD looked at the blade in Diaz's hands. They'd risked so much to protect it and might not be so lucky next time. He grabbed it out of Diaz's hands and threw it to the floor as hard as he could. It thudded, as if landing on a soft pillow.

"What are you—"

He stamped on the blade. Still nothing. He looked around for something that he could use to destroy it. His eyes landed back on the club lying on the floor. It was heavy, made from stone, just what he needed.

"Please, no," Diaz said, standing between JD and the blade. "It needs to be studied, understood."

"It needs to be destroyed," JD said.

"He's right," Milly said, stepping away from Tom. "They can't get it. This blade can be used to bring back a god of demons; we can't let it fall into the wrong hands."

Diaz closed her eyes and then stepped away, her hands held up in surrender.

JD lifted the club above his head and brought it down with all of his strength. A purple light blasted out of the blade and the club shattered as if it had been made of clay.

The Blade of Shadows lay on the floor, not so much as a scratch on its dark surface.

"Well, how about that?" Connor said.

Diaz bent down to retrieve the blade.

JD covered it with his foot before she could touch it. "Professor," he said warningly.

"I know," Diaz said, "I know. It has to be destroyed. But the question is, how? So if you would let me examine it?" JD lifted his foot so that Diaz could pick it up. She held it to the light. "Interesting."

"What is?" JD said, grateful of the distraction.

"This symbol." She angled it so that JD could see the engravings on the hilt. "It looks like the symbol for a key."

"Can't we just, like, chuck it in Lake Michigan?" Connor said, gesturing over his shoulder.

Niv held his hand up and signed dropping something.

"Yeah, or drop it in a volcano?" Zek said.

"Do you see any volcanoes around?" Tom said.

Zek shrugged.

"I will call my contacts in Mexico," Diaz said, handing the blade back to JD. "Maybe one of them will have heard of this."

"Okay," JD said. "And until then, we will keep it safe."

When they arrived back on the upper floor of the museum, the party was over. Only a few cleaning staff were buzzing around, sweeping up broken glass and crushed canapés, as the boys filed out of the exit with Milly and Diaz.

They all stood at the top of the stairs, looking down on the plaza below.

"To think", Diaz said, running her fingers through her hair and untangling the bun it had been in, "these things I have studied my entire life, these gods and mythic beings, are not so mythic after all."

"Quite the rush, hey?" Connor said, hitting Diaz with his full-watt smile.

"What? Oh, no, I much prefer my books. In fact, I am going to go home now and consult them. See if there's anything that might be able to explain what I've seen tonight. Even for a mind as agile as mine, it's been a lot to take in."

"If you find anything…" JD reached into his suit jacket and pulled out a business card, one of the few he carried for moments just like this. It had their real contact number on it. "And thank you, professor," JD said. "Without you…"

"I was lucky," she said with a shrug. "We all were."

They said their goodbyes and headed back to the jeep, which now had a yellow parking ticket stuck to the front.

"You might think they'd let you off when you're busy saving the world," Zek said, peeling it off the window.

He threw it to Niv, who added it to the collection in the glove compartment. Niv would hack the system later and this ticket would vanish.

Zek drove, with his brother in the seat next to him. Connor leaped into the boot seat, while JD and Tom sat in the back with Milly between them.

"So," Connor said, leaning over the seat and squeezing his head between Milly and Tom's. "We killed the bad guys, got the evil blade of doom or whatever, and saved the girl!"

"Oi!" Milly said. "I think you have that the wrong way around!"

Connor winked at her. "You know what this calls for?"

"A party?" Zek said.

"A party!" Connor grinned.

JD forced a smile as the other boys whooped. They'd seen Mourdant turn to dust before their eyes, Zyanya had vanished and they had the blade. And yet, JD was pretty sure that Tezcatlipoca wasn't finished with them quite yet.

He looked at Milly, who was staring out the window.

She wasn't smiling either. He reached out his hand and took hers. She didn't resist, interlacing her fingers with his.

Grit rattled against the bodywork as Zek slammed on the gas and drove them home.

Falling for you

The shower wasn't hot enough to scrub away the dirty, dark feeling that coated Milly. No shower in the world would be. Not even bathing in lava would do it. She could still feel the beast's blood on her hands. The shock of what she'd done was fading and the guilt was pouring in. She tried to tell herself that she'd had no choice. It was the demon or JD. But it wasn't working. As well as that, she kept thinking about the expression on her mother's face in that moment. No, she told herself, *Zyanya's* face. Her mother was gone. Dead.

Was it true? Had they really defeated the priestess tonight? The boys were celebrating, but she couldn't help feeling that it wasn't over.

After twenty minutes of standing in the increasingly cold water, Milly finally gave up. Pulling on fresh clothes, she wrapped her old ones up in a bundle, and then hesitated before picking up the blade. She hadn't realized she'd taken it into the shower with her. She placed it inside the bundle of her clothes and went to join the others.

Tom was playing his keyboards and singing. Milly recognized the song as the one she'd heard on TV what seemed like a lifetime ago. Tom's voice wasn't as strong as JD's but it was still good – sweet and clear. Connor hung, upside down, off one of the bunks, drumming on the floor, while Gail pounded her stick along in time. Meanwhile, Zek and Niv were in some kind of hip hop dance-off, each pulling off moves that the other would then try and beat. Zek was good, but Niv was the clear winner.

JD sat in a corner, gently strumming on his guitar. A part of things and yet somehow distant from the others.

Milly watched them as they sang, laughed and danced and she felt the tension finally start to lift. If they were so confident that the nightmare was over, maybe she should believe them.

Tom was the first to notice her. "Milly! Come and join us!" He put the keyboard aside and patted the sofa next to him. Milly sat down, sinking into the soft seat.

"I hear you saved my boys tonight," Gail said.

"I don't know," Milly said, looking down at the bundle in her lap. She hadn't recognized herself earlier. After she had killed the Jaguar Warrior, all she had wanted was to keep on killing. She hadn't known she had so much rage inside her

– it was like the Blade of Shadows had somehow brought it all out.

"You should have seen Slugger, Gail. She was like, *bam!*" Connor said. "Totally saved JD's backside."

Slugger? Milly thought. She'd been called worse.

"She was…amazing," JD said.

Milly's cheeks glowed at the compliment and she felt warmer than she had standing in scalding hot water.

Niv gestured fluidly and even though Milly didn't quite follow it all, it was still beautiful to watch. He was signing something about a blade.

"Can I see it, Milly?" Gail asked.

Milly blinked a few times at the use of her name and looked up. She dug around in her bundle of clothes and pulled out the knife. It was so beautiful. She liked the way it was no colour and all colours at the same time.

Gail nodded encouragingly towards the black blade. "Milly, can I see it?" Gail asked again, snapping Milly out of it.

"Oh, right," she said, placing it down on the table in front of her. "Sure." As soon as she let go of it she felt more together, more herself.

Gail picked it up and turned it over in her hands. "Obsidian with a bone handle."

Could be human, Niv signed.

Milly felt suddenly sick. "Human?"

Niv patted his arm, pointing to his humerus bone. It sent a shiver down Milly's back.

"Diaz is looking into ways to destroy it," Tom said.

Although she knew it was the right thing to do, Milly felt a strange sadness at the idea of destroying something so beautiful. "But what if it's useful?"

"It certainly worked on the jaguwere," Connor said.

"The what?" Zek asked.

"The snarling thing that nearly killed JD. Half-man, half-jaguar. Jaguwere," Connor said, looking pleased with himself.

Zek just shook his head.

"Until we know what we're dealing with, no one is to touch it," Gail said, standing up and crossing the aisle of the bus. She pressed her hand against the wall and a section swung open. Inside was a set of shelves filled with all sorts of weapons and tools. She dug around and pulled out a silver briefcase, about half a metre long. Instead of locks there were two smooth panels on either side of the handle. Gail pressed her thumbs against them and they lit up. A blue light beaded along the length of the panels, scanning Gail's thumbprints, and then the case clicked open. Gail placed the blade inside and closed the lid.

"It stays with me from now on. No one is to so much as look at it again till I say so, okay? We're working on nothing but theory and guesswork," Gail said. "And I don't like it."

"But Mourdant is dust!" Connor said. "And he was the mastermind behind all of this, right?"

"You killed his host, yes. But a demon as powerful as him can sometimes…" She drifted off, as if an idea had occurred to her.

"'A demon as powerful as him can sometimes' what?" Tom said. "I hate it when you do this."

"Nothing. I'll worry about Mourdant another time. For now, we have to find Zyanya."

"That shouldn't be too hard," JD said. "Without Mourdant, she's just a regular demon."

"I'd hardly call a demon priestess 'regular'. How many times do I have to tell you boys: d—"

"Don't get cocky!" the five boys chimed and they all laughed.

"We did good though, Gail," Tom said. "Can't we just enjoy tonight?"

"He's right, Gail," JD said. "For once. We can get back on Zyanya's trail tomorrow."

"Can we have just one glass of bubbly, Gail?" Connor said. "Please! It doesn't even have to be the good stuff."

Milly remembered the last time she'd drunk champagne and suddenly the inside of the bus felt too hot. Too full of people. She stood up and pushed past Zek, almost knocking him to the floor.

"I need some air," she said, throwing the door open.

It was raining. The bus hadn't moved from under the railway bridge, where they were safe from prying eyes and, according to Niv, prying CCTV. A curtain of water fell over the edge of the bridge, running into drains that were already overflowing. Milly sat down on the bus steps and closed her eyes, letting the air cool her face. Her head buzzed like an untuned radio. Too many thoughts. Too many voices. She couldn't make them stop. Demon priestesses and Jaguar Warriors. Blades and summonings. A few days ago, the only thing she'd had to worry about was whether someone would steal her homework. Now, everything she thought she knew about the world was gone, like someone had untied the bowlines on her life and it had all drifted away. She was lost and she didn't know how to find herself again.

"You okay?" Tom stood in the doorway, one hand resting against the frame, the other tucked into his pocket, like he wasn't sure if he should have followed her. But she was grateful.

Tom was the only one who had made her feel truly welcome in the strange group. Connor and the twins tried, but she wasn't sure how comfortable any of them were around girls. As for JD, he was still so unreadable.

She shrugged in reply.

"Sorry, dumb thing to say," Tom said, sitting down on the step next to her. "How can you possibly be okay right now with all of this? But you will be okay. I promise."

"My feet hurt," Milly said, wiggling her toes on the step.

"Heels will do that, or so I'm told. My mother called them instruments of torture."

"She wasn't wrong."

Tom laughed. "She loved them though. I still remember the delight on her face when she would open one of those white boxes and slip on a pair of new shoes and make me dance with her. And the look of pain when she came home later and threw them across the room."

"I think I'm more of the throwing kind of girl than the dancing."

"Here, give me your foot." He reached his hands out and Milly hesitantly placed her foot in his palms. "I'm pretty good at foot massages."

He wasn't lying. As he worked his thumbs into the ball of Milly's foot, she felt the pain ease away.

"What happened to your mum?" A look of pain flashed across Tom's face. "You don't have to tell me, if you don't want to."

"No, it's all right," he said. "My mum was a model, when she was younger. She met my dad when she was only eighteen and he was nearly forty. He was this big movie star and I guess they fell in love."

"A movie star?" Milly asked.

"Kit Wills? He was big in the eighties."

"Your dad was Kit Wills?" Milly said excitedly. "The action star? I've watched all of his films."

Tom laughed. "Well, that's more than I ever did. He walked out the day I was born. He paid for my education and sent me cheques on my birthday, but that was all I ever had to do with him. He died in a plane crash when I was ten. Turns out he had a gambling problem and so there was no money left. After that, Mum sunk into a kind of depression. For a couple of years she would hardly leave the house. But then one day, her friend came over and told her about this new pill that would fix everything. She'd be happy, look young again, and could even have her modelling career back. The pill was called Possession."

"Oh, no," Milly said.

"Oh, yes. So you can guess how that went. I was there the day it happened. Of course, I didn't know that it was a demon that was trying to kill me. I still thought it was my mum…"

Milly realized what he was saying. "Oh, God, Tom. I'm so sorry."

"It's okay, I guess. Gail arrived in time and saved me. She then set it up to look like my mum had OD'd." He stared out at the rain. "Sometimes I forget. Like, I catch myself thinking, *Oh, I must tell Mum about that*. It's been two years and I still think I see her in crowds."

"It's the same with my dad. JD said it never goes away."

"He might be right. But I guess it becomes a new normal."

"I don't think my life will ever be normal again."

They sat in silence watching the rain ease up and eventually stop. Tom gently swapped Milly's right foot for her left, and she became very aware of the feeling of his hands on her skin.

"Thanks," she said, retrieving her foot. "That's better."

"Any time."

Silence stretched between them and Milly felt the need to fill it with something, anything, to distract herself from the butterflies dancing in her stomach. "You know, I get being in a boy band. I even get fighting demons, now I know they exist. But both?"

Tom considered this. "Do you know what it takes to fly all around the world tracking these things down? What it really takes to go up against them?"

Milly tried to think of an answer. "A death wish?"

Tom laughed. "No, I meant money. A butt-load of cash. The weapons, the vehicles, the tech. Fighting evil doesn't really come with a pay cheque, so Gail had to think of something that would. She'd been in a band when she was young, before…"

"Before what?"

Tom opened his mouth as if he was going to explain. But then, with a small shake of his head, he changed his mind. "Just before. So when it came to making money, that's the one thing she knew how to do."

"But now you have the money, why not quit the band?

It can't be easy balancing these crazy lives."

Tom rolled his shoulders back, stretching out tired muscles. "Because we love it."

His smile was infectious and Milly couldn't argue with it. "But don't you ever wish you could just walk away?"

"To what? I don't have anything except the boys and Gail and Agatha." He patted the side of the bus.

"You don't want a home?"

A look of sadness passed across his face. "Sure, one day maybe. When I'm ready to settle down. Wife, three kids, a dog."

"I'm allergic to dogs," Milly said, and then choked, realizing what it had sounded like.

Tom smirked. "I'll remember that."

They both watched the rain for a little longer.

"You were really impressive back there," he said. "In the museum."

"I've never so much as thrown a punch before."

"You've never been in a fight?" Tom asked.

"I was in one." Milly thought back to when she'd been caught in a corner by a particularly vicious school bully. "But only on the receiving end."

"Well, we have to do something about that."

Tom stood and gave Milly a hand up. He led her onto a small patch of grass growing in the shadow of the bridge. She wriggled her bare feet on the damp ground.

"What are we doing?"

"I'm going to teach you how to throw a punch." Tom grinned.

"Can you teach me to block too? Like in the movies?" Milly threw her arm up and made a "*Waaaa*" noise like she'd heard fighters make in kung fu films.

Tom laughed again. "Sure. Only not like that." He stopped Milly windmilling her arms around. "Basics first," he said. "How to stand."

Tom started showing her how to place her feet, before moving onto attacking moves. "When you don't have much strength, you have to compensate with speed and surprise. Use your elbows, your knees. Anything to give you an edge." He talked her through elbow punches, knee strikes. "If you're fighting someone bigger than you, you have to get in close. Use their strength against them. Here, let me teach you a throw."

He stood behind Milly and put his arm around her neck. She could smell the clean talc scent of his deodorant.

"So, um, try and throw me."

Milly twisted this way and that, trying to tip him over. But she only succeeded in making Tom laugh a lot.

"First, you need to grab hold of my arm really tight. Okay, then bend forward, pulling me off balance."

Milly did as instructed, so that she felt Tom's weight against her back.

"Now turn!" Tom said.

A moment later, Tom landed on the muddy ground with an "*Oof!*"

Only Milly forgot to let go, so she came tumbling down on top of him. Their faces were barely centimetres apart. A strand of her hair brushed against the side of his cheek. He reached up and tucked it behind her ear, and a small smile twitched at the corner of his mouth. His lips parted and she felt his breath on her skin. The world narrowed to the space between their lips. It grew smaller, smaller...

"Her stance was all wrong."

Milly jerked her head up to see JD leaning in the doorway, arms folded. How long had he been there?

Flustered, she quickly rolled off Tom and clumsily pushed herself upright. Tom jackknifed back onto his feet in a move that she could have sworn was meant to impress her. It worked.

"Better than when you first started, JD," Tom said, brushing some dirt off Milly's shoulder. "You should have seen him when he first turned up. He was so bad. He used to just charge at me, all snarls and flailing limbs. Rebecca used to call him the mongoose."

"Rebecca?" Milly asked.

"The woman who taught us to fight," JD explained, jumping down off the steps. "Gail met her back when she and her band were on tour in Israel."

"Tiny little thing, but, boy, was she fast."

"Yeah, she kicked our butts over and over till we got it right."

"It just took a little longer in JD's case," Tom said, punching his friend playfully on the arm.

"I can take you down, Tommy boy, and don't you forget it!"

Tom held his hands up in surrender. "He's right. What JD lacks in technique, he more than makes up for with aggression. Isn't that right, mongoose?"

Lightning-fast, JD wrapped his arm around Tom's neck and pulled the boy into a headlock.

"I give. I give!"

JD knuckled Tom's hair and then released him.

"Well, come on then," Milly said, bristling a little from JD's criticism. "If you're so good, you show me."

JD looked Milly up and down, and she felt the brush of his gaze almost physically.

"All right then, let's see what you've got."

Milly placed her feet the way Tom had told her – a shoulder's width apart. JD took a step closer, and then another. He was shorter than Tom, but broader, his muscles more defined. Whereas Tom had made it all feel like a game, JD's intensity unsettled her. When JD looked at her, it felt like he was looking deep into her soul, really seeing her in a way no one else ever had.

JD walked around in a circle before coming to stand in front of her again, even closer this time. His eyes were light grey and he had a small mole on his left cheek, just above his dimple.

"So," he said, and Milly felt her stomach clench as he looked her up and down again, "what would you do if an attacker came at you like...*this*." JD lunged, grabbing hold of Milly's neck.

Without thinking, Milly lashed out, burying her fist into JD's stomach. JD's eyes widened. His mouth dropped open. Then he made a soft, mewing noise, before crumpling to the ground.

"Oh my God, I'm so sorry." Milly dropped to her knees next to JD, who was now rocking back and forth in the mud. She'd hit him in self-defence, but she hadn't meant to hurt him. "JD, speak to me."

She looked to Tom for help, but the other boy was also curled up in a ball on the ground. For a moment she panicked that she'd hurt him too somehow, then realized he was laughing. "Stop it, Tom, I think I really hurt him."

"He was all...*let's see what you got*...and you..." Tom couldn't speak for the laughter. "You... *Bam!*"

"Stop it!" Milly got to her feet and kicked Tom in the ribs. Only gently. It was bad enough that she'd hurt JD.

Tom managed to get his laughter under control and clambered to his feet. "It's okay, he's only winded." Tom crouched down and helped JD sit up. "Come on, JD, breathe through it."

JD nodded, and slowly the colour returned to his cheeks. "I'm okay," he said, waving Tom away and getting to his feet. "Just give me a second."

"JD, I am so sorry," Milly said, "I don't know what happened, I just reacted."

"Yeah, pretty good reactions, I guess," JD said, his arm still wrapped around his stomach.

Tom looked from one to the other and burst out laughing again. A moment later, Milly was laughing too and finally JD joined in.

"Have you lot finished beating each other up?" Zek's head appeared through one of the bus windows. "Diaz is on the line." He gestured for them to come back inside.

Milly climbed the steps behind JD, who was pulling off his muddy T-shirt and revealing a toned body. She tried to avert her eyes, but it was proving tricky.

"Have you found something?" JD asked as they stepped inside.

Diaz's face was on three of the video screens. Behind her glasses, her eyes were bloodshot. "I think so."

Milly sat down in front of the screens and stared up at the professor.

"I just spoke to one of my Nahua advisors from the excavation of Teocalli-Ome."

"Teocalli-Ome?" JD whispered to Milly.

"The pyramid she was excavating," Milly answered quietly.

"He is one of the last remaining Aztec descendants and his people have heard of the blade. It is said to be carved from a shadow and blessed by Tezcatlipoca. It's virtually indestructible."

"I still say volcano is the way to go," Zek said.

"I said virtually," Diaz said. "There is one way."

"Go on," Gail said.

"It can be destroyed by the first ray of sunlight that rises over the *Teocalli-Ome* pyramid."

"I thought pyramids were Egyptian?" Connor said.

"Step-pyramids were built by the Aztecs too," Zek said. "Which you would know if you bothered to pay attention in school."

"We don't go to school."

"Fair point," Zek said.

"Can you two shut up so Diaz can talk?" JD said. "Okay, so we get the blade to this temple and we wait for sunrise."

"But it has to be the dawn of spring equinox, the first day of the new cycle of Quetzalcoatl."

"Which is?"

"Two days from now. And, because the Aztecs worked on a fifty-two year cycle, this is our last chance to destroy it for decades."

There was a pause as they all processed the information.

"Zyanya will try and get the blade back," Zek said.

JD nodded. "So we'll have to destroy it before she does."

"I guess we're off to Mexico then?" Tom said, smiling.

"Hi, this is Gail Storm." Their manager was already on the phone, the silver briefcase still in her hands. "Yes, *that* Gail Storm. I need to book a private jet."

Flying high

When they had arrived to catch their flight at Chicago's O'Hare airport the next morning, there was already a gaggle of fans screaming their names and paparazzi flashing their cameras. Gail sometimes leaked their locations to get their pictures in the press. Which was one aspect of their lives JD could really do without.

He'd pulled his beanie down low and climbed out of the jeep. Tom waved at the gathering like he always did, smiling as if it didn't bother him that they barely got a moment's privacy. Connor waved too and high-fived a few of the fans, leaving them swooning in his wake. Zek and Niv stared straight ahead as if there was no one there but the two of them, and cut past all the chaos without so much as a blink. And Gail smiled from behind her large, dark glasses, which meant that no one saw that the smile didn't go anywhere near her eyes. JD wished he could be more like them, but he blinked at every flashing bulb and winced when his name was screeched over and over. Despite what Gail kept telling him, he would never get used to it.

It looked like Milly was finding it all hard to handle too. She walked behind them, twitching and blinking as the crowd screamed and cameras were pushed into her face.

"Who are you?" a journalist shouted. "Are you dating someone in the band? Are you married to JD?"

One girl grabbed Milly's arm and yelled at her: "You can't have Slay. They're mine! THEY ARE MINE!"

"No…I'm not…" Milly tried and failed to explain herself to the screeching fan.

"Come on," JD said, wrapping a protective arm around Milly's shoulder and pulling her away. "It will be over soon."

"Thanks," Milly said, flinching as another camera flash went off. "I thought my mother had it bad, but this is next level. Where's a toilet to hide in when you need it?"

JD laughed, strangely glad that at least he wasn't alone in hating all the attention. "Didn't I tell you it's insane?"

They made it into the relative quiet of the private departure lounge. The airport had been warned of their arrival and they were quickly rushed through passport control and immigration. A man had turned up at Agatha first thing this morning, holding a brown envelope that contained a brand-new passport for Milly under a new name. JD never asked Gail how she managed to do these things. She also had ways of avoiding security, which meant that, along with their instruments, they'd also been able to carry on a variety of weapons, and one silver case containing an ancient Aztec blade. Gail hadn't let it out of her sight since she'd locked it in there.

A G5 Gulfstream waited for them on the runway, along with two flight crew. A local team would already be setting things up for their concert.

"I'm Captain Delaney." A tall woman of about forty stood at the top of the steps leading into the plane. A peaked blue cap sat on top of an immaculate bob. "My crew and I would like to welcome you on board."

"Thank you for coming out at such short notice," Gail said, shaking the woman's hand.

"My pleasure, I'm a big fan."

"That's wonderful, isn't it, boys?" Gail turned to JD and the others.

She'd ingrained in them the importance of remaining grateful to their fans. They nodded and thanked the pilot.

"Sorry, no, I meant a big fan of yours, Ms Storm. I saw The Cyclones play at Clontarf Castle in ninety-two. You were phenomenal."

JD smiled when he saw a faint blush on Gail's dark cheeks. It wasn't often that she got the chance to revel in her old fame.

"That's very kind."

"Please," Captain Delaney said, stepping out of the way and waving Gail and the others inside.

The interior was like every other private jet JD had been on. Cream leather and tasteful down to its last stitch. A smiling flight assistant offered him a canapé from a silver tray as he walked down the aisle.

"No thanks," he said, quietly taking a seat and buckling his belt.

Zek plucked one off the tray and popped it into his mouth, then grinned.

Niv held up his index finger and waggled his hand from side to side, his expression quizzical.

"I don't know what it is. Tastes good though. Kinda fishy."

Zek grabbed another delicacy and, before his twin could complain, he'd shoved it into his brother's mouth. Niv looked put out for a moment and then started chewing. He nodded in agreement. It was good. The twins took the tray and sat down, quickly devouring mouthful after mouthful.

Connor had his head stuck through the cockpit door, most likely trying to persuade Captain Delaney to let him fly the jet. Or at least jump out of it at some point.

Tom sat down in the seat facing JD, watching Milly as she took a seat at the back. It was hard not to notice the way Tom looked at Milly. The way he blushed when they touched. JD should be happy for his friend. He *would* be happy for his friend, even if he had to force himself. Even if he had to ignore the twisting feeling he got every time he saw them together. He wasn't jealous, he told himself. He was only worried about what would happen when the time came for Milly to leave. They hadn't discussed what would happen with Milly when this Blade of Shadows stuff was all over, but she couldn't stay with them and JD didn't want Tom getting hurt. At least, that's what he was telling himself. He was only looking out for his friend.

"If you're going to make your move, you'd better get on with it."

"Move? What move? I have no moves. I am moveless," Tom said, blushing to the roots of his curly hair.

"Oh, please, you're all moves. 'Don't worry, you're safe,'" JD said, imitating his friend.

"Is that meant to be my accent? You sound like Prince Charles."

"Nice try, changing the subject," JD said, laughing.

"I don't even know what subject I'm supposed to be changing," Tom replied, still pretending to be clueless.

"Milly," JD said.

"What about her?" Tom said, glancing over at her.

Milly was staring out the window, listening to music on Tom's old phone.

"You like her."

"Maybe." Tom picked at a thread on his jumper. It was

black and white and had been hand-knitted by one of their fans. The fan had made them all jumpers, but Tom was the only one to wear his.

"And she likes you."

Tom's head snapped up. "Do you think so?"

JD ignored the acid taste at the back of his throat. "I think so. But, Tom, look…"

"What, don't you like her?"

"Of course I do, it's just—"

"She saved your life."

"And I will never forget it. But—"

"But what?"

"But nothing. I'll stay out of it. Just don't do anything stupid. More than usual anyway."

"I'll try." Tom looked back over at Milly.

JD had seen Tom go up against all kinds of monsters and yet he didn't think he'd ever seen him look so nervous. "Well, go and talk to her then."

"I don't know. You're right, now is a terrible time. I can't believe I was even thinking about it. She's just lost her mother."

"And if nothing else, she needs a friend."

"A friend, right. I can be a friend." Tom started to get out of his seat, then sat back down again. "If you say anything, I will kill you."

JD mimed closing a zip across his mouth.

Tom finally got up and JD twisted around to watch as his friend pointed to the empty seat in front of Milly. She took her earphones out and waved him to sit down with a smile.

Zek took Tom's place. He looked over at Milly and Tom and back to JD. "So."

"So what?" JD said.

"It's okay, JD. It's good. Healthy. You know, we were worried you'd never have feelings for another human. That you might actually be a robot."

"What feelings? I don't have feelings. I don't *do* feelings."

"Come on, JD, I've seen the way you look at her, so why don't you tell her? This isn't a romance novel. You don't have to bow out and 'do the honourable thing'. You can, shocking as this might sound, let Milly make her own decision."

"Seriously, Zek, I have no idea what you're talking about. Shouldn't you be having this little chat with Tom?"

"Tom isn't the one with a problem expressing his feelings."

"Look, I like her, sure, but as a friend and that's it. And if I have any 'feelings' it's worry about what we're facing when we get to Mexico."

Zek stood and held his hands up in defeat. "Okay, okay, whatever. But you know... When your programming. Permits you. To access. Your emotion core..." Zek made jerking robotic movements.

"You will be the first one I come to," JD said.

Zek joined Connor and Niv at another of the tables,

leaving JD to himself. They all knew him well enough to understand that sometimes he needed his space. And now was such a time.

"Welcome aboard this private flight number 3780b to Cancún International Airport. Flight time will be approximately three hours and fifteen minutes. So please buckle up, as we're about to…*take off*."

With that, music started playing over the sound system. Heavy drums and loud guitars. It wasn't till Gail groaned and covered her face that JD recognized the song. "Take Off". It was one of The Cyclones' numbers.

The rest of the band all caught on after the first verse, and started singing at the tops of their lungs, much to Gail's annoyance. They knew the song as well as one of their own and even Milly knew it well enough to join in on the chorus. It had been The Cyclones' only song to hit the charts and yet it was Gail's least favourite.

"It was the nineties, okay!" she kept saying after every particularly cheesy chord riff or wail from her.

"I'm gonna fly you to the moooo-oooon and back," Connor wailed, completely off-key. It was lucky he had rhythm.

The song came to an end with a pounding double kick of the bass drums. Gail took a bashful bow in her seat as the boys clapped wildly. JD laughed, his tension fading as the engines started up and they took off.

He looked out at the city below them, the houses and shops getting smaller and smaller till they were like models on a train set. He didn't know what awaited them in Mexico, but for now, for the first time since they'd rushed to Milly's house, JD felt like they were finally one step ahead.

A song for you

Milly had never felt more in the way. Everyone else moved like a cog in a well-oiled machine: roadies unloading the instruments; stage crew erecting the set; electricians running back and forth with cables and lighting rigs. While Milly contributed absolutely nothing. Unless gawping could somehow be considered constructive, and she was pretty sure it couldn't.

They'd set up in Valladolid, a small town five hours' drive from Teocalli-Ome – the pyramid in the heart of the jungle Diaz had told them about. The first day of the spring equinox was tomorrow, so they'd travel to the temple late tonight and be ready for the dawn that would destroy the Blade of Shadows, and with it the chance that Zyanya could complete the ritual to bring back Tezcatlipoca.

Where was the demon priestess now? she wondered. Most of the boys seemed to think she'd been defeated back in the museum, Diaz's symbol banishing her and turning her to dust like they'd seen happen to Mourdant. Milly wasn't so sure. The demon who had killed her mother was still out there, she sensed it somehow.

But one thing at a time. Destroying the blade was the most important thing. Then she could go hunting for Zyanya.

She'd spent the afternoon wandering around the town, enjoying the feeling of the heat on her skin. Sun-faded buildings painted in ice-cream pastels nestled next to sweeping colonial arcades. The narrow streets were lined with taco stands, craft workshops and men and women selling a never-ending variety of fruit and vegetables. Women in sharp outfits that wouldn't look out of place in New York or London chatted with women wearing traditional dresses embroidered with flowers as bright as their smiles. Milly bought an iced coffee from a stand and took a seat on a bench in the central square. A large Mexican flag flew in the light breeze, with the image of an eagle crushing a snake in its strong talons in its centre. Nobody paid her much notice as she sat and watched people come and go. Around the square, scooters wove in and out of brightly coloured taxis and vintage cars. Milly even saw a man on horseback clip-clop down the limestone streets. No one seemed to be in a rush. Apart from Slay. They had a show to put on.

With a population of just 50,000 people, Valladolid wasn't exactly on the tour circuit – which, Tom had explained, meant it was exactly the kind of place Slay loved to play.

"We do this," he'd said earlier. "Put on gigs with only a day's notice. The fans seem to love it – they have forums dedicated to checking our every move to see if we might be about to announce another one. And as soon as the word goes out, they go wild! It's fun. And it gives us the excuse to go anywhere we're needed."

The concert was going to be held outside the Convent de San Bernardino de Siena, a pink-walled fortress located just on the edge of town. They were expecting over five thousand people to turn up that night and Milly could feel the air of anticipation take over the quiet town.

Milly didn't understand how it was even possible to put on a performance of this size with only a few hours' notice. But the roadies were well used to it. And by the time she'd finished her stroll and joined the boys at the Convent, the stage had been built and the lights turned on.

Now she kept being told to get out of the way by grumpy, bearded men. Milly had been told the roadies were chosen because they could be trusted with the band's secrets. But she wondered if they'd actually been chosen because of how terrifying they were. Wherever she ended up, she'd only be moved on again by another grumpy, bearded man.

She started to wonder if it wasn't just the same man making fun of her.

She finally found a spot, halfway up a lighting rig, from where she could watch events without being shouted at. Below her, the band was in the middle of rehearsing a cover song they'd decided to add to the set. They bickered about harmonies and when the drums should kick back in. But when they started to play, something magical took hold. It was like the five of them could read each other's minds – each one bouncing off the other, adding their own particular touches to the song.

It must feel amazing to be a part of something like that, she thought. Her whole life, Milly had always felt out of sync with everyone else. As if the rest of the world was zigging while she was zagging. Up in this lighting rig, feet dangling, she felt it more than ever. She was just a spectator in these boys' lives. She was even, now she thought about it, a spectator in her own life. Always overthinking, overanalysing everything. The only time she felt free was when she played music.

Without really thinking about it, she found her fingers dancing on the edge of the rig, playing an invisible piano. She could hear the notes in her mind, a harmony to the song the boys were playing. She longed to be back at her piano at home, where she could hear the notes for real. The song finished and the boys seemed satisfied that they had it down tight.

Milly found herself humming the chorus, which had already earwormed itself into her head. JD and Niv wandered offstage to go and check the sound quality from the back seats, while Connor thrashed out a drum solo.

"You okay up there, monkey girl?" Tom peered up at Milly on her perch.

"Oh, sure, fine. Some guy threatened to rip my arm off if I got in his way again. So I thought I'd be safer up here. Good acoustics too."

"What do you think now you've heard us live?"

"I liked it! Catchy, like a virus. Only you know…a good kind of virus, not the kind that makes your face melt off." Milly wanted the rig to collapse and take her with it.

Tom laughed. "Well that's good, because I have a favour to ask."

"Sure, anything."

"You play piano, right?"

"Yeah but…"

"No buts!" Tom said, waving her down. "Get down from there and come and help me work out a song that's stuck in my head."

Milly shimmied her way down the rig, but got her feet tangled on one of the last rungs.

"Here." Tom grabbed hold of her waist and lifted her gently onto the ground.

"Thanks," she mumbled, pulling her T-shirt back into place.

She followed Tom out onto the stage. As she did, the lights slammed on, blinding her. She lifted her arm to cover her face. "Are they always that bright?"

"Yeah, apart from when they turn them all off for the laser shows."

"How do you see?" Milly tripped over a cable and stopped herself from falling by grabbing hold of a mic stand.

"You don't!" Tom laughed at Milly's confused expression. "But we know our way round the stage so well now we don't need light. See."

To prove his point, Tom closed his eyes and walked confidently towards the piano, pulled out the stool and sat down. He opened his eyes again and smiled at Milly. "Come on, sit down."

Hesitantly, Milly sat next to Tom. The stool was only just big enough for the two of them. Their bodies were pressed closely together and Milly became acutely aware of the humidity and a bead of sweat trailing down her neck. She wasn't the only one affected by the heat. Droplets gathered on Tom's top lip, which he licked away.

Milly swallowed hard and turned her attention to the piano. It was an electric Yamaha GT20, a world away from the classical pianos she'd played her whole life. She laid her fingers on the keys and let the weight of them play a chord. The sound was amplified through all the speakers spread around the plaza, making it feel like the notes were coming from within her bones. It echoed over and over, the one chord reaching all the way to the back of the arena.

"Nice, hey?" Tom said as Milly gazed around in wonder.

"It's incredible."

"Now, I've had this riff stuck in my head for days. But I can't work out what to play next." Tom's fingers danced across the keys, picking out a series of notes. They sounded familiar and yet fresh at the same time. He hummed along with the chords and then suddenly stopped. "And I don't know where to go from there."

"Play it for me again," Milly said.

As Tom did, Milly stretched her fingers out on the keyboard, gently brushing Tom's fingers.

"How about something like this?" She played Tom's opening melody and then added a series of notes.

"Nice!" Tom said. "Zek, get in on this."

Zek swung his bass guitar over his shoulder and wandered towards the piano, his head tilted as he listened. He started to pluck his guitar strings, the notes layering over what Milly and Tom were playing. Milly looked up and smiled as she heard the snap of the snare drum and the roll of beats: Connor laying down the rhythm.

"*You never know where you'll hide them,*" JD's clear voice rang out over the PA system.

Milly twisted in her seat to see JD with the mic in one hand and Niv's battered notebook in the other.

Niv stabbed at the page, shaking his head.

"Oh, right," JD said. "*Find* them. Your handwriting is terrible."

Niv stuck his tongue out, then plugged his guitar in and started to strum.

"*You never know where you'll find them, like a jewel waiting in the dark*," JD sang again. "*And before you know it, they've made their home in your heart.*"

What started out as a couple of chords slowly grew and grew: chords, rhythm, lyrics, all finding their place. The song was about making new friends and knowing they'll become old friends. Milly had written songs herself, pieces for the piano, things she would hum to herself. She couldn't really describe what happened when she made one up. It felt as if the music was out there, floating in the air, and she was just discovering it, like her mind was a radio receiver just picking up the notes. But writing with the band, this was something else. If writing songs on her own was like tuning into a signal, this was like catching a wave.

She felt the hairs on her arms stand on end. Milly let the last chord hang, the notes ringing out and floating up to the blue sky. As the sound faded away, they all knew. They'd just made something great.

"Wow," Tom said, looking at her. For a moment they were alone, on the stage and in the world. Just her and Tom and the lingering echo of the song they'd made.

"You know, maybe, when this is all over, you and I could…"

"Could what?" Milly said, feeling her heart pound a little faster.

"Write some more songs together?"

"Songs. Oh, sure," Milly said, realizing that was even better than what she thought he'd been about to say.

"That was deadly!" Connor said, splashing a cymbal as he jumped off his stool and over the drum kit. He slammed both hands down on Milly's shoulders and shook her, shattering the moment and nearly pulling her off her seat. "Pure deadly."

"It was pretty good," Zek said, slipping off his guitar strap.

"It was better than pretty good," Tom said quietly. "We make a good team, Milly."

Milly smiled. "We do."

I wrote the words for you, Niv signed.

"Thank you," Milly said, putting her open palm to her chin and pulling it away, making the sign for gratitude. "They're beautiful."

"You know what? We should play it tonight," Tom said.

Connor whooped in agreement while Niv and Zek nodded.

Then slowly, one by one, they all turned to JD. A dull thud, as he placed the mic back in its holder, echoed through the sound system. Milly couldn't read JD's expression. She felt a connection with all of the boys after the moment they'd just shared, but JD could still be so distant.

The singer turned to her, his head tilted, and again she felt that penetrating stare of his boring into her.

"Sure," JD said, the line of his mouth breaking into a bright smile. "Why not?"

Tom hesitated for a moment, before pulling Milly into a hug. She felt the sandpaper roughness of his stubble against her cheek. Connor suddenly wrapped the two of them up in his arms and before Milly had a chance to move, he pulled them all to the floor with a shout: "Pile on!"

Milly felt the weight of a third and then fourth body throw themselves onto the huddle and finally JD joined in. It was hot and sweaty and she had Connor's knee in her ribs and Zek's armpit in her face. She couldn't breathe under the weight of them. And yet for some reason, Milly felt if not exactly happy, then something close to it.

Don't leave me waiting

Ten minutes to go before the show. Ten minutes and the crowd was already screaming in anticipation.

"*Te amo*, JD! *Te amo!*"

JD knew the words for *I love you* in over seventeen languages. And no matter how many times he heard it, or saw it scrawled on sheets of cardboard and held in tiny, tight hands, he would never get used to it. He knew it wasn't really him they loved, but rather the *idea* of him. The boy in the poster on the wall. The boy who sang to them as they fell asleep at night. If they knew the real him – the grumpy, shy kid who didn't like meeting new people – JD didn't think they'd feel the same. Not to mention how they'd react if they knew about the demon-hunting stuff.

But none of that mattered, because tonight, Slay had a show to put on. Adrenaline bubbled in his bloodstream, clutching at his stomach, making his mouth dry. Every time he went out onstage there was always the moment when he thought he would freak out and run offstage. Even as he walked out into the darkness before the blinding lights came on, he was never totally sure that tonight wouldn't be the night where it all went wrong. Maybe that was part of the reason he felt so euphoric when it was all over: the sheer relief of getting through it. Sometimes he wished they didn't have to bother with the charade, that they could just stick to fighting demons and forget about the music. It would make life so much simpler. Simpler, he thought, but a lot less fun.

He picked up his Gibson Hummingbird and slipped his arm through the strap. It had been tuned by the roadies already, but he couldn't resist a final check himself. He ran his fingers up and down the strings, enjoying the buzzing sigh they made. It was his favourite sound in the world. Maybe he had it the wrong way around. Maybe they should give up the demon-hunting and just stick to the music. But how many more people would die if they did? People like Milly.

He heard the shuffling of the other boys around him as the crowd quieted in anticipation. As always, Connor walked on first. The fans erupted in whoops and cheers as he took his seat behind the drum kit and started pounding on the bass drum. The twins strode on next, waving at the now ecstatic audience. They plugged their guitars in and started strumming. Tom was next. The screams were almost deafening as he took his place behind the keyboard and played a few chords. JD took a deep breath and held it, then stepped onstage.

If the screams had been loud before, they were nothing compared to the noise pouring off the crowd now. It sounded like a jumbo jet taking off.

JD rested his hand on the mic, looked to the other boys, and nodded.

"One, two, three, four!" Connor shouted, clashing his sticks together at the same time. On the fourth beat the lights went up and the world exploded in sound.

They always started with "Home Is Where You Are", the song that had been their breakout hit. Its upbeat lyrics and irresistible bassline always got the crowd going. JD couldn't remember how many times he'd sung it now, and yet he never got bored of it. As he and Tom harmonized on the chorus – "*Don't need no roof when I have your smile, don't need no walls when you're in my arms*" – JD felt all the nerves flow away. They moved onto "While You Sleep" without a break, the sound of the crowd surging again as they recognized the intro. This was JD's personal favourite, mostly because he got to sit back during the verse and let Tom and then Zek do the singing. True, their voices weren't as strong as his, but JD thought theirs sounded sweeter. He always saw beauty in the flaws. He was almost sad when it came to an end and it was his turn in the spotlight again.

He unclipped the mic and walked to the front of the stage. "*Hola, Valladolid!*"

The crowd roared in response.

"Are you having fun? I said, are you having fun!"

Not everyone would understand his English, but they responded anyway. If there had been a roof, they would have raised it with their voices. He scanned the crowd, drinking in the adoration. He could feel the love pouring off them and into him.

"Thank you for welcoming us here today. On behalf of Tom…Connor…Niv…Zek…" JD paused after each introduction, allowing each boy to perform a quick solo. "And myself, JD, I thank you from the bottom of our hearts. But now, back to what you all came here for. The music. What shall we play next?" He turned to the other boys as they pretended to discuss what song to play.

"'Be My Baby, Baby'?" Tom said, and the crowd cried out in agreement.

"'The Road Keeps On Callin''?" Connor suggested to yet more screaming.

"Nah! It has to be 'Hit Me With All You Got'!" Zek shouted and the crowd went wild.

"Hit Me" was the first track the boys had ever recorded. They'd released it on YouTube and that's where it'd all begun. And yet they'd never played it live before tonight. It was clear the audience were as hungry to hear it as the boys were to play it.

"Oh, they don't want to hear that one," JD said, teasing their fans just a little. Just enough to get them riled up. "Well, if you're sure?" He grinned and strummed the opening note.

It was a perfect performance. They broke out into a jam towards the end that had the audience pounding in delight. He even saw Milly dancing away in the wings. The songs along with the minutes blurred into each other and by the time they finished "Blood on My Hands" the stars were shining in the moonless sky. The noise softened a little when they played a cover of the song that had been Connor's mum's favourite. Not many of their fans knew the words to sing along – although they picked up the chorus soon enough and were belting it back at them on the third revisit.

"And now," JD said as the applause died down, "we have another new song we'd like to play. It's a song about new friends and how you find them in the strangest of places. And for this, we would like to invite a new friend of ours onto the stage."

A hush settled on the crowd as the spotlight picked out a point in the wings. It had taken some work to convince Milly to join them onstage, but Tom had managed it in the end. She'd been standing there just a moment before, ready to come on. Now, she was gone. Maybe she'd chickened out? JD could hardly blame her if so, not with all the screaming fans waiting to judge her. In fact, if the girl had any sense she'd be hiding in the dressing rooms. JD would give her one more chance.

"Our friend is a little shy, so maybe if you could all give her a warm welcome onstage?"

The crowd responded with a deafening round of applause. But still the dark spot in the wings remained empty. And then he saw a pair of golden eyes glowing in the darkness.

And JD knew that Milly wouldn't be joining them onstage that night. She might, in fact, never be joining them again.

Hello again

Milly had been watching the gig from the safety of the wings, a VIP pass around her neck. She'd been backstage at hundreds of her mother's shows, but this was something else. While her mother's performances had been met with respectful silence and rewarded with loud applause, fans of the boys had been screaming from the moment the lights went down. And Milly couldn't blame them – the boys sure knew how to put on a show.

JD was a totally different person from the moment he walked onstage; all his coldness and spikiness melted away and he positively glowed with happiness. He charmed the crowd with his gentle chat, talking to them like they were up on the stage with him and not squashed between thousands of other fans. It was clear why he was the lead singer – it was hard to take your eyes off him.

Tom's transformation was less extreme – he was still the

same warm, friendly Tom, but Milly saw how the thrill of the performance overtook him. How it seemed to light him up from within. Niv and Zek too became bigger, better versions of themselves. And Connor, well, watching him drum was the first time Milly saw the boy properly relax. All of that twitching, untamed energy poured out of him and into the drums.

There was no other word for it. It was magical. Seeing them live was a completely different experience from listening to their album on Tom's old phone. She couldn't believe that she would be joining them onstage tonight. Nerves and excitement swirled in her stomach. She wasn't thinking about the Blade of Shadows or demon gods. For the first time in her life, she was in the moment.

She found herself singing along with the fans to "Hold On Tight", and even though she was in the wings, Milly felt part of the crowd. As if they were all one huge family united by their love of this music. The walls of the town shook with their voices. As the boys burst into "Whenever I Close My Eyes", Milly smiled out at the audience. Mobile phone screens shone in the coming twilight, faces gazed up at the band, lost in complete adoration. But one face in the middle of the crowd wasn't smiling. One face wasn't loving the show.

Zyanya. She was here.

Milly felt like a great block of ice had slid into her stomach.

She'd known it, even if she'd hoped so hard that it wasn't true; she'd known that Zyanya was still alive. And now the priestess was here for the Blade of Shadows.

Milly looked across the stage, past the boys, to where Gail stood, the silver case by her feet. Well, Milly thought, Zyanya was going to have to go through her to get it.

She and the demon priestess locked eyes across the bouncing heads of the audience. Zyanya smiled.

Milly didn't think. She didn't plan. She just ran. She didn't have a weapon or training. All logic was wiped away by a raw, primal hatred. All she knew was that she had to get to Zyanya.

A roadie grunted at her as she barged past him, throwing herself down the stairs that would lead out into the pit. She leaped over scaffolding and slid under black curtains until she was standing below the stage, a small barrier and some large men between her and the crowd.

As everyone else was pushing forward against that barrier, in the vain hope of getting closer to the stage, Milly pushed back the opposite way. Jumping over the barrier, she squirmed and elbowed her way through the mass of bodies, every now and then catching a glimpse of plaited dark hair bound in golden thread. It seemed to be moving further away from the stage, heading for the edge of the crowd. Milly was getting closer, closer, not caring that she knocked a small girl off her feet as she clambered to get past.

Finally, she made it to the edge. Bursting through the last row of people, she came face-to-face with the demon possessing her mother's body.

"Ah, my child."

"I am not your child!" Milly spat. Her fists were curled in balls so tight her nails were cutting into the flesh of her palms. She was going to use those fists to punch and pound. She drew her arm back, ready to let fly as Tom had taught her. A hand with a grip like iron clamped around her wrist, dragging her away from Zyanya. Milly looked up to see a man wearing a black T-shirt stretched across tight muscles. She was sure she recognized him – he'd worked at the opera in Chicago. What was he doing here? He smiled, revealing a row of sharp pointed teeth and Milly understood. Zyanya had turned another human into a demon puppet.

Milly yanked and twisted her arm, trying to get away, but the demon's grip only tightened. She whimpered in pain as she heard bones crunch.

"How nice of you to come to me, Milly," Zyanya said. "Offering yourself up. I'd call that willing, wouldn't you?"

"Willing? But…"

"Take her," Zyanya said. "I will join you there once I have the blade."

The demon dragged Milly away, wrapping an arm around her stomach and lifting her off her feet. A few people glanced over as Milly called out for help, but they turned away.

To them, Milly was a crazed fan being dealt with by security. If only they knew what danger they were in, the danger the *world* was in. She screamed and screamed, but her warnings were lost in the shouts of the crowd and the music of the band.

The demon holding her put a thick hand around her throat and squeezed. Lights danced at the edges of her sight until darkness closed all the way in.

Bring it

The crowd was still cheering for Milly, but slowly they were becoming aware that something else was going on. Most of them thought it was all part of the show. Slay were known for throwing in a few surprises, after all.

JD looked back to where he'd seen the golden eyes glowing. Three men stood in the wings. As he watched, their faces warped and stretched till they were completely unrecognizable as humans. Straight white teeth buckled and grew into sharp points, limbs bulged and grew black-spotted fur, and fingers rippled and grew razor-sharp claws. More of Zyanya's Jaguar Warriors. Demon beasts summoned to protect their priestess.

His reflexes twitched, ready to fight, but his first priority, beyond even protecting Milly or the boys, was to protect the fans. He picked out one face in the crowd: a young girl with glossy tears of joy pouring down her plump cheeks as she stared up at JD. They couldn't fight the creatures in full view of this many people, not without causing utter chaos.

"Stage fright," JD shouted to the others, covering the mic with his hand.

There was barely a moment's delay as the four other boys processed the meaning of the code phrase and sprang into action. Gail too was ready. She flicked a switch and lights spun around to point at the crowd, the stage flooded with dry ice and laser beams pulsed around in circles. A track of one of Slay's songs blasted out at even higher volume. All just disorientating enough to hide what was about to happen from the audience.

Now that he didn't have to worry about revealing their secret to thousands of people, JD focused all of his attention on the sets of golden eyes to his left. He kicked the mic stand free of its base and, with a flick of a button, released the spear hidden within. Tom reached under the keyboards to pull out a small crossbow. Connor tossed away his drumsticks and grabbed a new set from the holder – these were made from titanium and sharpened to a deadly point. Niv and Zek threw down their guitars and picked up matching bright red ones from the stand on the stage. They didn't bother putting them over their shoulders and instead held them by the neck, like baseball bats. If anyone actually tried to play these guitars they would have been in for a nasty surprise.

The boys had never been attacked onstage before, but Gail had made sure they'd always be ready.

The five boys formed a line, JD in the middle, Tom on his right, Connor on his left and the twins on the ends. The Jaguar Warriors charged. The first only made it a few metres before Connor threw one of his sticks. It sliced through the air and into the Jaguar Warrior's heart. The demon roared in rage but kept coming, right into the path of Niv.

The twin swung the guitar with all his might, his mouth open in a silent scream. The instrument crashed against the creature's head and chest, red wood splintering and flying in all directions. But the wires didn't break. They kept on, slicing through its flesh, through its neck, till they passed out the other side, cleanly removing head from body. Because this guitar hadn't been strung with ordinary strings, it had been strung with razor wire.

The head bounced on the stage floor, its golden eyes open in surprise, and the body slumped and toppled forward.

One down, two to go. The second Jaguar Warrior hesitated after seeing his friend dispatched with such little effort.

"Bring it, you hairy goat-lover!" Zek shouted, hefting his guitar-come-club over his shoulder. It looked like he was hoping to match his brother's truly monumental takedown.

The Jaguar Warrior snarled, the drool dripping from its maws like liquid mercury in the black light. JD wondered if it would back off – it must know it was outnumbered. But fear clearly wasn't part of this thing's make-up – or logic, for that matter. It leaped straight at JD. JD jumped too, meeting the creature in mid-air. His spear slashed, meeting little resistance, and by the time he landed, one knee bent, his arm holding the spear stretched out behind him, there was another dead beast lying on the floor.

The final beast sprung high into the air, leaping right over their heads and landing behind them. Before the boys could change formation, Gail burst out from the wings, her long limbs flick-flacking over each other as she pulled off graceful one-legged cartwheels. She came to a stop, her bad leg stretched out to the side, her good leg bent low. She held her stick loosely in her left hand; the scabbard was off and the sword was out. She whistled, as if calling to a dog. The beast reared up and roared at her. JD didn't even move. He knew Gail could more than handle herself against one of those things. Hell, she could have probably taken on all three of the beasts while the boys carried on with the show. Even with her injured leg and her missing eye, she was a formidable fighter.

The beast swiped at her, its claws slicing through her T-shirt. Her blade flashed in a figure of eight. *Slice, slice, slice.* One more disposed of.

JD peered into the wings, checking for any other demon beasts – and that's when he saw her. Zyanya stood there, clapping slowly, her arms stretched towards him as if she was offering up her applause to the boys. Then she stepped back into the shadows and vanished into the darkness.

They'd been so stupid to underestimate her – to think that she was powerless without Mourdant. Well, they wouldn't make that mistake a second time. But first, the show. The fight had taken less than two minutes. He could sense the crowd starting to get nervous, worried that the gig had come to a sudden end. He was desperate to chase after Milly, but if JD and the others didn't reassure them that everything was okay, they might have a riot on their hands.

The roadies, who had been hand-selected because of their own experiences with demons but who were under strict instruction to stay out of demonic fights for their own safety, rushed on and dragged the bodies away. A loud clapping and stamping started up in the crowd.

"We ready?" JD called out to the group.

"Born ready," the four other boys replied in unison.

The lights turned back to the stage and the crowd roared in appreciation. "Sorry about that technical hitch," JD said, trying to keep the aching anxiety out of his voice. "But we couldn't leave you without saying a 'Last Goodbye'."

Cries of joy and disappointment poured out of the crowd as they realized this would be Slay's last song of the night. It was always the last song they played. JD sang as the others joined in, harmonizing. He pushed back the fear that tightened his vocal cords and twisted his stomach. Connor played just a little too fast, as eager as he was to finish; Niv strummed his guitar so hard he broke a string. They were all fighting to stay in control.

When the last note came to an end, JD flung the guitar off his shoulder and threw it to the floor. "Thank you, Mexico!"

The show was over.

You, alone

When Milly came to, there was only darkness. She couldn't move her hands or feet, and rough material chafed her cheek. The material was damp from her exhalations, which made it hard to breathe. A cloth bag over her head, she reasoned, and plastic ties around her wrists and ankles.

She twisted her wrists in the bindings, but it only made the pain worse as the sharp plastic sawed at her skin. Milly cursed all those hours she'd spent studying; cramming her head with quadratic equations, Latin puns and learning the difference between stalactites and stalagmites. What use was any of that now that she was tied up in the back of a truck and about to be sacrificed to a demon god? She'd taken so much pride in knowing as much as she could, in reading everything she could get her hands on. And for what? To please her mother, who hardly noticed she existed?

An old resentment bubbled up, twisting at her insides as

sharply as the bindings did her wrists. If her mother hadn't always been chasing her next big shot, if she'd cared more for her daughter than she had fame, then she'd never have been seduced by Mourdant, and Milly wouldn't be all alone and being taken who knew where.

Don't think about that now, she told herself. *Focus. First things first,* she thought, trying to calm the panic clutching at her heart, *where are you?* She felt the hum of an engine through her bones. She must be in a vehicle and, judging by the way she was being thrown around, they were moving at top speed over very rough roads. She had no idea how far away she was from Valladolid and the boys. She hoped they were alright, that they'd fought off Zyanya. They had to be alright. For now, she had to worry about herself.

She ran through her options and they were pretty limited. She was trussed up and ready for sacrifice. She remembered Diaz's description of the ritual of Tezcatlipoca, how the sacrifice would have their heart cut out. In the darkness, the image of Alice's face flashed through her mind. Was that how she was going to end up?

No. Whatever Zyanya might have said about Milly being willing, there was no way Milly was going to give up without a fight. While she was still alive there was still hope. If only there was a way of sending a message to the others...

"You idiot!" she said out loud when she realized how stupid she'd been.

Tom's phone was still in her back pocket. Now, if only she could get to it. She was almost grateful to whoever had tied her hands behind her back, because it meant she could easily reach her pocket. She pulled the phone out and cursed when it slipped through her damp fingers and fell to the floor with a clatter. She patted around trying to find it and, at last, felt the cool glass under her fingers again. She'd turned the phone off when the show was on, so she pushed the power button, wishing she could see the reassuring light of it coming on. When the starting noise chimed, she thought it was the sweetest sound she'd ever heard. She slipped the phone back into her pocket. Now, she just had to hope that the boys would have the same idea as her. If they didn't...

The vehicle came to a sudden stop. There was the sound of a door rattling, opening. She pressed herself against the cold metal wall, wishing that somehow she could pass through it. Footsteps. Her hood was lifted. She blinked in dull light, looking up at the man standing over her.

He looked normal enough, apart from the shimmering golden eyes. He had thinning black hair and a nose that had been spread flat across his face.

"Please, you don't have to do this. You can let me go. I know you're kind, you probably have a family waiting for you. I know you're not this...this thing."

"Oh, you *know*, do you?" The man laughed a dark,

sickening laugh. "Think you're clever, do you? You don't know jack."

The flicker of hope in Milly's chest died.

The man reached into a bag behind him, pulled out what looked like a white sheet and threw it by Milly's feet. "The priestess wants you ready when we arrive. Put it on."

It was a robe of some kind. Like the outfit she'd been forced to wear when playing the angel in her school nativity when she was six, minus the tinsel halo. She sniffed, hoping he didn't notice her snotty nose and watering eyes. She didn't want him to know just how scared she was.

"How am I supposed to put it on with my hands still bound, genius?"

The man grunted and pulled out a switchblade. He flicked it open and bent down so he was nose-to-nose with Milly. She could feel the tip of the knife resting against her chin.

"Now, put it on, or I will make you. Do we understand each other?" Milly nodded as best she could without puncturing her skin on his knife. He moved away and spun her around. She felt pressure on the bindings and then the tightness around her wrists gave.

"Ah, now what's this?"

Milly turned to see Tom's mobile phone in the man's hands. He dropped it and smashed it under his heel. Milly felt like he'd crushed all her hopes with it.

"Think you're clever, do you? Well, not too clever for me."

She'd need to think of another plan, and fast. She rubbed her wrists, the pain spiking as the blood flowed back to her fingers. The man waited while she pulled the robe on over her clothes – there was no way she was undressing in front of him. It swamped her, the hem gathering on the floor, the sleeves falling way below her fingertips. And it smelled like a wet dog.

"Happy now, clever clogs?" The man walked towards her, holding out the sack that had been over her head.

"Ecstatic."

And everything went black once more. Her hands were bound again, tighter than before. The van doors slammed and a moment later the engine rumbled to life. Milly was thrown to the floor as the van screeched off into the dark.

Get you back

As the squawk of the dropped guitar died, JD raced to where Gail waited in the wings.

She grabbed JD's face, twisting it into the light, checking for injuries, patting him up and down. She checked each of the boys in turn, before finally returning to JD.

"We're all fine," he said, taking hold of her hands. "But... Gail..." He looked down at a gash in her T-shirt. "You're bleeding."

"I'm fine, it's a scratch. What happened?"

"Zyanya was here, and...I think she has Milly."

"And the blade." Zek pointed at the empty spot by Gail's feet.

Gail gasped and looked around desperately. "It was here... The case was right here."

"The fight was just a distraction," JD said, punching an equipment case so hard it rolled backwards. "How could we have been so stupid?"

"It's my fault," Gail said. "I should have stayed with the case. I should have trusted you with the fight. But it's done. Right now, we need to focus. Zyanya has the Blade of Shadows."

"And we have to get it back before sunrise tomorrow."

"How?" Tom said, chewing on his lip so hard he'd already drawn blood. "We have to find her...we can't..." He couldn't even finish.

JD wanted to reassure him, wanted to promise that they would get Milly back whatever it took, but he didn't even know where to begin. Zyanya had a good few minutes' start on them. She could be anywhere.

"Wait!" Tom said. "My phone. I gave Milly my old phone."

"Niv, can you track it?" JD said.

Niv pulled his phone out and flicked through the apps. He punched the buttons and they all waited anxiously as *Searching... Searching* flashed across the screen. With a ping, a blue dot appeared on the map.

"Yes!" Tom said. "She's not far. Less than a mile away."

JD smiled and patted Tom on the shoulder.

"No, wait, what's happened?"

The blue dot had disappeared from the screen.

"Maybe they found the phone," Zek said.

"She was heading east, maybe we can work out where they were taking her," JD said.

"To Teocalli-Ome," Connor said.

"But isn't that the same place we have to be to destroy the blade? Why would Zyanya take it there?"

"It's to do with the eternal struggle. Light and dark, life and death. Tezcatlipoca and Quetzalcoatl. Diaz said the temple was shared by the two gods. Tonight, it belongs to Tezcatlipoca. But after the sun rises tomorrow, it belongs to Quetzalcoatl for another fifty-two years. So tonight is her last chance."

"Since when did you become an expert on Aztec temples?" Zek asked, looking at Connor in surprise.

"I downloaded Diaz's book. It's really fascinating. Did you know that—"

"Enough talk, you have to go aft..." Before Gail could finish, she collapsed.

JD caught her and helped her sit down, propped up against a speaker. Only then did he see just how deep the wound Gail had called "a scratch" was. It was bleeding fiercely.

"You need to go to hospital."

Gail pressed her hand against the cut and winced. "You may be right. But you need to go after Milly."

"We can't leave you," Connor said, kneeling down beside Gail.

"This isn't open for discussion. Milly takes priority. Carl!" she shouted.

One of the roadies rushed over. As soon as he saw Gail's injury, he went pale behind his beard. "Oh, my."

"Call an ambulance and, oh, get the bag."

Carl nodded and a moment later came running back with a large black bag. JD recognized it as the bag containing their weapons. "Ambulance is going to be too long. I'm taking you." Carl threw the bag to JD and scooped Gail up in his thick, tattooed arms as if she weighed nothing.

"There's a black van outside." Gail dug a key out of her pocket and threw it to JD. "Now, go!"

JD watched Carl and Gail vanish backstage and then, with a look to the other boys, he ran. The other roadies began packing up, which tonight would include disposing of the bodies of the Jaguar Warriors. Carl was the best roadie they had and JD knew Gail would be safe with her. She had to be.

He paused at the exit, waited for the others to catch up, then yanked the door open. Niv slammed it shut and grabbed him.

Niv looked troubled. He slapped his palms together and made a clockwise twisting motion, as if squashing something.

"He's right," Zek said. "We'll get crushed out there if the fans see us."

JD zipped open the holdall and peered down at the collection of blades. "No masks."

"We don't have time to find them," Tom said. JD had

never seen his friend so afraid. He too felt a panic he'd never come close to feeling before. He couldn't bear to stand around talking for a second longer. It might already be too late for Milly.

"Perhaps we need a different kind of mask," Zek said, eyeing up a cardboard box by the door. He ripped it open, revealing a stack of Slay merchandise. He threw T-shirts and caps at each of the boys, before pulling off his own shirt and replacing it with one that said *EAT, SLAY, LOVE*.

"The perfect disguise," he said, holding his arms out. "Fans!"

JD had to give it to Zek. No one would expect a member of Slay to actually wear a Slay tee. As long as they kept their heads down, they could just blend into the crowd. JD yanked a *I ♥ SLAY* T-shirt on over the one he was already wearing and threw open the door.

They moved quickly through the people pouring out of the concert, without getting so much as an annoyed grunt from people they had to shove out of the way. In fact, it was amazing how many of their teen boy fans were dressed exactly like them, with their hair styled in the same way. Some even had tattoos drawn up their arms to match the boys' ink. He'd have to remember this for the next time he wanted to wander the streets without being spotted.

"There!" Connor shouted, pointing ahead at a black van parked between two of the six-wheeler trucks that had carried all their gear. It was unmarked and ready to go.

JD threw the keys to Connor, who snatched them out of the air and clicked the doors open. Now wasn't the time to bicker over who'd drive and although he was the youngest Connor was the best behind the wheel.

They all clambered in and buckled up. It was six hours till sunrise. Six hours to get to the temple, stop the ritual and save the world. Six hours to save Milly.

Connor started up the van and they sped off into the night, not knowing if they would ever see another dawn.

Don't keep me hanging

Milly had no idea how long she'd been in the back of the van. Minutes slipped into hours. Time lost all meaning. Finally, the van slammed to a halt. Parched, hooded and tripping over the long robe, she was dragged out of the vehicle, up some stairs, over a hot sandy floor, through what felt like a tunnel and then down a rough slope. All the time, she felt the knife pressed against her neck by the jaguar-man who insisted on calling her "clever clogs". One wrong move and she'd be dead. She ran through various escape plans in her head. But when it came down to it, she wasn't trained for any of this. She wasn't JD or Tom or any of the boys. She was Milly. And she was scared.

The golden-eyed man threw her against a solid, cold wall, wrenched her hands above her head and strapped metal cuffs around them. Then Milly heard footsteps walking away. And a door slamming closed. The bag clung to her face, her sweat and saliva sticking it in place. She sucked in a mouthful of the material, ignoring the fact it tasted like feet, and tugged at it with her teeth. It gave, just a little. She repeated the process again and again, till finally, the bag slipped off her head. She spat it out onto the ground and stamped on it a few times for good measure. Now she could see again, she took in her surroundings.

A large room, illuminated by the flickering light of candles. The walls were lined with... Milly blinked to make sure she was seeing it right. Yes, they were lined with skulls. She twisted around, trying to see as much of the room as possible. It was a square room built from large stone slabs placed one on top of the other so perfectly that you could hardly see the gaps. Milly had to give it to the people who had built this place, they sure knew a thing or two about angles. But even their precision had been worn down by the pressure of time. The ceilings were low and held up by three square pillars and, in one corner, a metal prop. The entire room looked like it might collapse at the slightest provocation. Death by sacrificial ritual or crushed by rocks. Not a choice she was willing to make.

"Ah, my child." Milly recognized the voice only too well. Zyanya walked through a narrow doorway and down the rough steps, running her hand against the skulls embedded in the walls.

"Don't do this, please let me go, *Ma*—" Milly said, feeling a gut-punch of sadness as she almost used the word for "mother".

Having to see her mother's body still walking around, looking into her mother's eyes and seeing only darkness, made it almost impossible to accept the truth. But she had to. Her mother was dead.

"Oh dear, still holding on to the hope that your mother is in here. So innocent. And I am afraid I can't let you go," Zyanya said. "We need you. And isn't that what you've always longed for? To be needed? To be wanted? To be loved?" The demon priestess reached out and stroked Milly's cheek.

Milly twisted away, growling. "You touch me again and I'm going to…"

"Going to what?"

"I don't know yet. But it's going to be really bad," Milly said, letting her head drop again.

The demon laughed. Milly didn't know if the glow in her black eyes was a reflection of the flickering candles or coming from somewhere deep inside her. "Before, we had no need of chains," she said, stroking the metal binding Milly's hands. "Before, when my people ruled this land, before the *Spaniards*" – she spat the word – "we would make a sacrifice to Tezcatlipoca every year. As a child, I would watch the ritual with wonder, as a beautiful young man would walk up the steps of the pyramid and put himself in the hands of the priests. Willingly giving his body over to the god. It was a great honour to be chosen. And the priests would open his chest and rip out his heart and set a fire in the place where his heart had been. And all the time, they sang. Oh, child, I wish you could have heard the singing. It was like the gods themselves breathing. When I was chosen to be a priestess and conducted my first ritual, you can't imagine the power I felt when I held the knife in my hands... never had I felt closer to another human being. But that, that was as nothing compared to the ritual I will finally finish tonight. There are no conquistadors to stop me. Tonight, Tezcatlipoca, the Lord of Shadow, shall walk again, and the world shall be made anew."

"You have no idea what you're doing!" Milly shouted, yanking on her chains. "Can't you see? Tezcatlipoca is going to use you and destroy you and then destroy the world. Which bit of 'god of death and destruction' are you not getting? If you summon him and let him into that body, you're gone. Dead. You get that, right? You won't be around to see this great new world of yours."

"Oh, but, my child, I won't be Tezcatlipoca's host. I will be the one who nurtured him, who gave birth to him. I will walk at his side as his mother."

"Mother? But...then who...?" Milly knew it before Zyanya smiled. "No...no, you can't. I won't be his host. I know the rules, you have to be willing, you have to invite the demon in. I won't."

"Wait, my child, you will see. Tezcatlipoca can be so persuasive. Everything you've ever wanted will be yours. Your every dream fulfilled."

"But I'll be dead!"

"Oh no, you will live on. Two souls entwined in one."

Milly didn't want to believe what she was hearing. The boys had told her that once a demon stepped in, the human soul was thrown out. But if the soul was still in there...

Zyanya tapped her heart. "Yes, your mother is in here, or an echo of her. At first she tried to fight, especially when she thought I was going to hurt you. It was quite distracting. Back in the museum, when I was weakened by Diaz's little game, your mother managed to drag me away to save you. I punished her for that. Whatever was left of her is broken. I am in control. But you will learn all of this for yourself, when Tezcatlipoca comes."

Tears flowed, coursing down Milly's face. "I will fight. You and your stupid god. You were stopped last time and you'll be stopped again."

"Silence!" Zyanya roared. It sounded like a thunderclap and felt like a punch to the face. "I will have my revenge! And those who dare stand in my way shall be crushed beneath the feet of my god!" Spittle flew, her black eyes bulged. She composed herself. "So, you see, there is no way out. You may as well submit quietly, like a nice little girl."

She smiled and made her way out of the chamber.

"Yeah, not my style," Milly said, once the demon was out of earshot.

The show can't go on

The black van rolled to a halt, kicking up a cloud of yellow dust. The gates guarding the pyramid site were brand-new and locked with a thick black chain. A fence ran around the perimeter and various warning signs told people to stay away in both Spanish and English, threatening trespassers with prosecution or, judging by one sign, electrocution. The area was thick with trees and vines. There was no way through for the van; they'd have to go the rest of the way on foot.

JD jumped out and adjusted the scabbard on his back. He waited as Niv cut through the wires electrifying the fence with a pair of cutters, and then began climbing. When he reached the top, he threw himself over, avoiding the barbed wire, and landed on the other side, knees bent, fingertips brushing the ground. One by one, the others followed, landing either side of him. Only Connor had trouble with the barbed wire, managing to leave a chunk of his T-shirt behind. But other than a nasty scratch on his back, he was okay. They set off, running down the track cut through the jungle that would lead to the ancient Aztec temple.

The area was overgrown and JD felt like they were being watched every step of the way. Stone statues stared out of the trees at them: figures with bird heads, snakes with gaping mouths and skulls with rolling tongues. Everything seemed like a warning to stay away. He heard the insistent hiss of cicadas in the distance and the howling of creatures he couldn't identify. The heat was almost tangible, as if even the air was trying to stop them getting to the temple.

As they got closer, he could make out grey, crumbling buildings breaking through the trees, all radiating out from a central square that was covered in grass. Up ahead, a step-pyramid cast a shadow across the ground in front of them. A flash of lightning picked out the jagged shape against the roiling, purple clouds. It looked like a stairway to another dimension.

"Well, I'm going to go out on a limb and say that's the temple," Zek said, pointing to the looming pyramid with his curved sword.

It was easily thirty metres tall, made from nine stone platforms stacked on top of each other. Perched on the very top was a small, square building with doorways leading inside. Carvings of plumed snakes and snarling jaguars covered the building, which was illuminated with flaming torches. JD couldn't tell if the snakes were chasing the jaguars or the other way around.

Crumbling staircases ran up each of the four sides of the pyramid. Three of the sides were still mostly covered in plants and grass as the nearby jungle tried to reclaim the building. But the central staircase was clear and waiting.

JD stopped at the base of the pyramid and looked up. And up. At the very top of the steep steps, a figure walked out of one of the doorways and onto the upper platform. She raised her arms, holding up something so black, so dark, it looked like a tear in the very air: the Blade of Shadows. Even from down here, JD could see she wore a huge feather headdress and a long cape of jaguar skin. Zyanya in full priestess regalia. He could say one thing for her, she knew how to make an entrance.

Behind her was a large slab that couldn't be anything other than an altar, and lining the four edges of the platform stood rows of hulking creatures. Their eyes glowed gold in the dark.

Connor spun his sais. "More of the jaguweres!"

"Stop trying to make 'jaguweres' happen, Con," Zek said, readying his scimitar.

JD drew his katana and adjusted his grip on the ray-skin hilt, feeling the heightening of his senses that came with the adrenaline rushing through his system. They were outnumbered ten to one by demon beasts with razor claws and shredding teeth. A demon priestess with an unbreakable blade had their friend. And they had less than an hour to stop the ritual. His brain was giving him two options: fight or flight? There was only ever one choice.

The five boys stood in a V formation with JD at the front, Tom to his right, Connor to his left and the twins taking up the rear.

"Sure," Connor said, "we've faced worse."

"Actually, I don't think we have," Zek said, spinning his blade around his shoulder. "But you know what they say?"

"No, Zek, what do they say?" Connor asked, his sais dancing between his fingers as easily as his drumsticks.

"When going up against an army of demons, the wise man wears brown trousers."

"Sometimes," Tom said, stretching out his shoulders, "I get the feeling you just make these things up."

"This", said Connor, "is going to be fun."

As JD placed his foot on the bottom step, Zyanya raised her hands to the sky, opened her mouth and began to sing.

Like a domino

Milly was smart. People told her that almost every day. Some meant it as a compliment, others not so much. She was a straight-A student. The best in every class she'd ever been in. But as she gazed around the chamber, she'd never felt dumber. This was one situation she couldn't think her way out of. She banged her feet against the rock in frustration and heard the stone creak. She looked up and tugged at the chains binding her hands. They were fixed tight, but the column itself was old and had been bearing the weight of the roof for hundreds of years. The metal support propping up the cracking ceiling looked frail, as if it was struggling under the burden of the stones. She looked from pillar to pillar, calculating the angles. It was a half-baked idea at best, and if her maths was out by even a little... But what other choice did she have?

She lifted herself up on her aching arms, twisted her

body around as much as she could, and slammed her feet against the metal brace. Nothing happened. She kicked again. Dust flew and the brace shifted a fraction. Milly closed her eyes, drew up all the strength she had and kicked again. The brace slid out of place and toppled to the sandy floor with a muffled clang. Milly waited. And waited. Then, with a sound like a stone coffin lid being opened, a crack appeared in the roof. And grew. It raced across the ceiling towards the pillar Milly was chained to. A fissure branched out of the crack and grit rained down. As slowly as an iceberg breaking off a glacier, the pillar itself started to shatter. Milly closed her eyes, hoping she wasn't about to get herself killed.

"Oh, sh—" she shouted as both she and the pillar went crashing into the one next to her. Like a giant row of dominos, each pillar smashed into the one next to it, till all that was left was a pile of rubble. Milly coughed, breathing in the dust, and rolled away from the heap of stones. It wasn't exactly what she had intended. She'd been hoping just to crack the column enough to free her chains, but it had had a slightly more dramatic effect.

"Ha!" she said, jumping to her feet. "Take that, everyone who told me not to waste my time on maths." She tried to punch the air, but her wrists were still bound by heavy metal links. The collision had shattered the stone holding her, but not the chains. One thing at a time. Dust fell from the ceiling and more cracks were appearing. She wouldn't have long before the whole place caved in. The only way out was through the door at the top of the room. Zyanya would surely have guards waiting somewhere beyond. There had to be another way out. A hidden door maybe? She moved around the room, looking for any helpful levers. Nothing.

"You'd think a place like this would have at least one secret door. What good is an evil Aztec chamber if it doesn't have a secret door?" It reassured her to say it out loud, made her feel like she was in a movie, talking for the benefit of the audience rather than living through this nightmare. The grinning skulls looked like they were laughing at her. "Yeah, I don't know what you think is so funny," she said to one. "You're dead."

She pulled torch brackets, pushed at carvings, anything that might be a hidden lever or button. Nothing budged. Which left only the door. She placed her bound hands on the door, readying herself. She had no idea what she would find on the other side.

"Ready?" she said, to her imaginary audience. "On three. One. Two. Three!"

Milly shoved the door open, expecting to find someone, or something, waiting. But there was nothing. Only a small corridor sloping upwards. Torches lit the way. She stepped into the tunnel, swearing to herself that if she made it out of here alive she was going to spend the rest of her life running through sunlit fields, like in yoghurt commercials. She'd always been told that she needed to get out more. *I promise*, she thought to herself, *I'll never waste a day indoors again.*

Like the walls of the chamber, the corridor was lined with skulls. Whoever had built this place really, really liked dead things. Skeletal heads peered down from alcoves dug into the rock, their empty eyes boring into her. In the torchlight, Milly could see symbols carved into the bone, similar to the marks she'd seen in Mourdant's diary: geometric patterns that made her head spin just looking at them. She tripped on the uneven ground and had to stop herself from falling by grabbing one of the skulls. Her fingers slipped inside its eye sockets and met something wet and squelching. She squealed and wiped her hand against her robe, telling herself not to think about what it was.

She'd never been more grateful when she finally came to another door at the end. Before opening it, she pressed her ear against the smooth wooden surface. Through it she heard the sounds of shouting, growling and screaming. That meant only one thing.

She turned to one of the skulls and grinned. "Just you wait. Slay are here."

Milly threw open the door and ran straight out into the arms of a demon with sharp teeth and golden eyes. "Well hello, clever clogs."

Let's dance

They were halfway up the steps. Torchlight reflected off Tom's bow as he dispatched demon after demon. Niv and Zek moved like tornados, slicing and dicing. Connor threw salt grenades blasting anything in his path. And JD spun and rolled, his silver blade flashing. It was almost like a dance. They all moved as one: fluid, furious and unstoppable.

Two Jaguar Warriors threw themselves at JD. With a smooth swoop of his blade, he took out one while Zek finished off the other. Another stopped in front of them, snarling stinking breath.

"You guys really need some mouthwash," Zek said.

It looked between the two boys, but before it could decide who to attack first, they struck. JD went high and Zek went low. The Jaguar Warrior's head went rolling down the steps, while its torso and legs lay where they fell. JD stepped over them and charged at the next attacker.

All the while Zyanya sang. Notes so pure and perfect that JD felt them wrap around him and lift him up. But the words…the strange twisted words she sang were anything but human.

He was maybe ten metres from the top platform when the singing stopped and was replaced with a cold, terrifying laughter. JD looked up to the altar and could see why. Lightning flashed again, illuminating Zyanya so perfectly JD wondered if it was coming from an overhead rig. It was her spotlight and this was her moment. She held the Blade of Shadows up, gazing at it with a look of utter adoration. Next to her stood Milly, held in the fierce grip of one of the Jaguar Warriors. She looked so weak, like a rag doll ready to be thrown away.

As JD started towards the altar, Zyanya's hand flashed. The blade stopped a centimetre away from Milly's heart.

"Drop your weapons," she said, her voice booming as if amplified through a sound system. "Or we will see how big this child's heart truly is."

JD hesitated, not wanting to obey the priestess's command. He'd come up against his fair share of demonic creatures: some were all charm and bright smiles, others were wild beasts, driven only by the desire to kill. But this one…this one was something else. For the past two years, Gail had been teaching JD about stage presence – how to own his place on the stage. But his whole life he'd never come close to the way Zyanya commanded an audience.

She was born to be onstage. Born to be adored.

They'd been fools to think that Mourdant had been the one in charge. Zyanya was the one with the power and she always had been.

"Drop them!" she shouted, pushing Milly against the altar beside her.

Milly barely moved. *Drugged?* JD wondered. *Or just beaten?* What choice did he have? He could cover the distance between him and Zyanya in a matter of seconds, but not before she could plunge the blade into his friend's heart. He lowered his sword to the ground. Tom and the others followed his example.

"Now bear witness," Zyanya said, "to the return of darkness!"

She dragged Milly onto the altar, the tip of the blade still pressed against her chest. The priestess began to sing again, ramping up the notes into her full range. What JD had heard had only been the warm-up. The words made him think of bubbling tar pits and nails scratching at coffin lids, screaming children and crying mothers. All hope leached out of him and all he wanted to do was curl up in a ball and wait for it to be over. There was no point in fighting. He was just a kid, a stupid kid who was never going to amount to anything. The voices of his teachers and care workers all came back to him, taunting, ringing in his ears.

"You're a bad boy, Joshua Deacon. You'll end up in jail.

You'll end up like your good-for-nothing dad."

Next to JD, Connor fell to his knees, sobbing, crying out for his lost family. Niv and Zek too had collapsed on the floor, hugging their knees, rocking back and forth. Only Tom stayed standing, fighting against whatever power the music had over the others.

"Fight it," Tom said, shaking JD by the arm. "Fight it. *When things get dark, don't forget...*" He sang the first line of "Hold On Tight", his voice clean and sweet.

"*I'm right beside you,*" JD picked up, adding his voice to Tom's. "*Nowhere you can hide where I won't find you,*" JD and Tom sang together.

As they launched into the song, JD felt the darkness lift. The images in his mind of all the times he'd failed, all the times he'd proved he was no good and couldn't be trusted, were replaced by memories of him and Tom and the rest of the boys, laughing, playing music, fighting side by side. He remembered the day they'd all gone to Disneyland and Connor had tried to steal a Goofy costume. The time they'd all played crazy golf in a snowstorm in Wales. The ritual had opened up a black chasm in his soul, which had threatened to suck him down into oblivion. But as Connor and then Zek joined their voices with his, the hole closed, breaking the grip of the demonic magic.

JD turned back to Zyanya, who had her eyes closed and her head held high. It was time for some payback.

I'm yours

Zyanya raised the blade above her head. It sucked in the grey predawn light, hungry to plunge everything around it into darkness. A bolt of blue-black lightning erupted from the rolling clouds above and struck the blade, crackling up and down from tip to hilt, illuminating the symbols carved into the hilt with a glowing black light. Zyanya screamed as if in terrible pain but the screeching turned to laughter. High, terrible laughter. Her hair stood on end and her black eyes shone silver.

"Accept the sacrifice of my Jaguar Warriors, slain in your name. Accept the body of this child as your willing host."

The blade flashed and Milly waited for it to be plunged into her chest. Waited for it all to be over. Zyanya's song had leached all hope out of her. But instead of thrusting it into Milly's heart, Zyanya used the blade to draw a large circle in front of her. Where the point of the blade passed, a glowing blue light appeared in the air, like a trail left by a sparkler. The symbol – the same one Milly had seen her mother cut into her skin – hung, suspended. It wasn't a light, Milly realized. It was a slice in the very air itself.

Through it, dark smoke poured like poisonous gas. Black tendrils crept across the stone floor and circled around the altar. The dark spirit of Tezcatlipoca was finding its way back to earth, answering the ritual's call. The smoke became denser and coalesced into the shape of a man standing over Zyanya. He was terrible. He was magnificent.

Zyanya stroked Milly's face with the flat of the blade, trailing it down her jawline and across her neck. Milly felt the coldness of the Blade of Shadows through her robe. Colder than anything she'd ever felt against her skin. But colder still was the shadow swirling around her.

Zyanya began carving a small circle through the white cotton into Milly's skin. The blade was so sharp that Milly didn't feel pain at first, just the wetness of her blood seeping into the material of her robe. And then it came, a hot searing agony that became her whole world. Zyanya stood back, as if looking at her handiwork. A small loop with overlapping ends lay like a pendant on Milly's chest. The mark giving Tezcatlipoca permission to take possession of her body. The mark that would make her his host.

The shadow spirit of Tezcatlipoca turned to Milly. Dark hands reached out for her, stroking the symbol cut into the skin below her throat. Milly wanted to close her eyes. She wanted to turn away from his touch. But she was frozen, arms bound, lying on the altar like a corpse on a slab. Zyanya sang what Milly sensed were the last words of the ritual. She could feel them vibrating in her chest and through her bones. She had only seconds before the god would possess her.

In that moment, woven under Zyanya's words, she heard something else. A soft humming, as if music was playing in another room. It became louder. Singing. Tom and JD's voices rising above Zyanya's.

Seriously, boys, Milly thought, *now is hardly the time for an impromptu gig.*

But as their voices became stronger, she noticed Zyanya's singing becoming weaker and realized its hold was waning. The demon priestess stuttered. It was putting her off. Zyanya shook her head as if to push out the words the boys were singing. This was Milly's chance.

She grabbed Zyanya's arm in her chained hands and rolled off the altar, taking the priestess with her. Not exactly like the moves she and Tom practised outside the bus, but it worked. She and the demon went crashing to the cold stone floor. The impact knocked the blade out of Zyanya's hand and it skidded away.

Milly dived for it, the fingertips of her bound hands brushing the bone hilt; she almost had it when nails dug into the flesh of her back and dragged her away. Driven by rage, Milly flipped onto her back, reached up and looped the manacle chain around Zyanya's neck in one swift move. They rolled, over and over, as the demon priestess tried to shake her off.

Zyanya stood, Milly clinging onto her back now, and Milly had a flash of memory of her mother carrying her like this when she was a child, while her father watched and clapped with joy. There had been laughter and maybe even love, although her mother had never used that word. Where had it all gone? When her father died it was as if he'd taken any happiness in either of their lives with him, leaving only a self-absorbed woman and an abandoned child.

Zyanya clawed at the chain, hissing and spitting. Milly's mother had been strong when alive and the demon that possessed her had given her body even more strength. She kicked off the altar, sending both of them crashing into the wall. The stone cracked under their weight and the wind was knocked out of Milly's lungs. But she wasn't going to let go. She clung on with every bit of strength she had as Zyanya slammed her into the wall again. Her head cracked against the cold stone and for a moment she saw stars. She shook them away and focused on tightening the chokehold, pressing one knee into the demon's back and leaning away, using her body weight to add to the pressure on the chain. Tom's voice came back to her: *Use anything to give you an edge*.

The creature that killed her mother gurgled and gasped.

"Do it, Lyudmila," a voice Milly recognized hissed through a crushed windpipe. "Please."

Milly froze as the realization hit her. Her mother was still alive, still fighting.

"I can't hold her back any more," Milly's mother said. "Do it! Save me. Save us both."

"I can't," Milly cried, loosening the chains.

Her mother's hands found hers and squeezed. "You have to. I love you."

In her entire life, Milly's mother had never said those words.

The voice changed again. "You cannot defeat me!" roared Zyanya, in control once more. "I will have my revenge!"

Milly knew what she had to do. She finally accepted there was no coming back for her mother, that she had to let her go. This was the only way to set her free.

"No!" Milly said, her voice choked with tears. "I will have *my* revenge."

She tugged with all her might, channelling all her rage, all her hatred and all her grief, tightening and twisting the chain around Zyanya's neck.

Finally, Zyanya went limp. The dead weight pulled Milly to her knees. Milly stayed there for a moment, panting, leaning her pounding head against the demon's still back. Then she unlooped the chain from around the neck and let the body fall the rest of the way to the ground.

Her mother's eyes – now brown once more – stared up at the grey sky. The demon was gone, leaving only an empty corpse. Milly threw herself on her mother's body, screaming, sobbing, the pain she had been fighting back for the last few days bursting out of her. But she couldn't break now, it wasn't over. She lifted her head and wiped away the tears.

The shadow god stepped forward, hands reaching out for her once more. The symbol in the air that had summoned him had faded. But there was one last part of the ritual still to be completed: Tezcatlipoca still needed to take possession of his host. The shadow god's body rippled with muscles, his eyes glowed silver; looking into them was like looking into a burning star. She was in the presence of a demon god – a being of pure power.

He's beautiful, Milly thought, *perfect. Why would I fight him? He's here to save me. He's here to save us all.*

"*No pain, no fear,*" a voice that sounded like worms eating corpses promised her. "*Only power. All can be yours.*"

If she gave in to him, became his host willingly, that power would be hers. She would be the greatest living thing on the face of this pathetic planet. Every person who ever snubbed her, she could crush. Everyone who ever abandoned her, she would destroy. And those who loved her, they would worship her. She would be adored. But, Milly realized, she would still be alone. Trapped for ever in a cage with a demon.

Tezcatlipoca moved closer, hands caressing the mark,

probing. Milly felt ice clutch at her heart. He was finding his way in, just as she'd seen Zyanya enter her mother's body.

"*Don't fight me, child. You have been chosen.*" The mark burned as if it was being carved into her skin for the second time. Hot blood flowed from the wound and the pain was all consuming. Colours pricked at the corners of her eyes and she felt a great weariness tugging at her consciousness. All she wanted to do was sleep. To escape.

She looked down to see the blade in her hands. She didn't remember picking it up. It felt warm and inviting. Powerful, but it was a different kind of power. The power of choice.

Milly didn't notice the battle going on around her as the boys fought to get to the top of the pyramid, to her. She was locked in her own battle with Tezcatlipoca.

Tom said that a human host had to let a demon in? Well there was no way she was letting this thing take her.

Sucking in a breath, she dragged the blade across the symbol carved into her chest, breaking the circle, denying the god his permission.

"I am stronger than you!" she shouted, ignoring the pounding pain. "That's why your priestess chose me, because I am strong. But you're weak. You're nothing but shadow and smoke, whispers in the dark. Well guess what, I'm not listening. No one is listening to you. So you can just go and crawl back to whatever hole you've been hiding in!"

The shadow form twitched and twisted as if Milly's words

were causing it pain. It shrank, getting smaller and smaller, until it looked like she was addressing her own shadow cast on the floor of the temple. She slashed through the chains binding her wrists and threw the blade to the floor, then opened her mouth to let out a victorious, "Ha!"

Before the sound left her mouth, the shadow spirit of Tezcatlipoca leaped. Shadow hands wrapped themselves around her throat, crushing, choking. One stayed on her neck while the other crept up her face, pushing into her mouth, her eyes, her nose, pressing and pushing and trying to find a way in.

"Wait!"

The god's hands froze.

A figure stood over Milly, the black blade in his hand. He was injured – a red mark on his arm that looked like teeth marks or…a looping circle hastily carved into his skin.

Tom smiled at Milly and said, "Take me."

Killer kiss

JD scooped up his sword and raced up the final stretch of steps, slashing, spinning, hacking at the Jaguar Warriors that stood between him and the altar. He'd stopped thinking and was acting on pure instinct; his only objective was to stop Zyanya and save Milly.

A Jaguar Warrior, which must have been easily 200 kilos, stepped in front of him, blocking his view. It pulled back purple lips to reveal sharp black teeth and roared fetid hot breath in his face. JD tried to dodge but it was too fast, kicking him in the chest and sending him flying backwards down the steps.

He landed on his back, hard. He didn't have time for pain. Jackknifing back onto his feet, he charged at the demon. At the last moment he skidded to his knees and spun, bringing his sword around in a smooth arc. The beast looked down at a gash that had appeared in its fur-covered stomach with a curious, almost hungry look on its face, before crumpling to the floor.

JD stepped over the body. Now there was nothing between him and the altar. He reached the final step, breath heavy and heart pounding, and saw Zyanya on the ground. Dead. A wave of relief hit him. It was over. The priestess was dead, the ritual halted. He glanced around, desperately seeking out Milly.

Then he saw her, on her knees before the altar, gasping for breath as a dark cloud swirled around her. The demon god was still trying to possess her, trying to force its way into her body. He raised his sword and hesitated. There was no way to stop Tezcatlipoca without hurting Milly.

"Wait!" JD heard Tom cry out, aching agony in his voice.

Tom stood beside Milly, the black blade in his hand.

No, JD thought. If it was too late for Milly, if she'd already been possessed, Tom shouldn't be the one to have to finish her. JD forced his limbs to move, but it felt like he was moving through deep, cold water.

"Take me."

What did Tom mean? He couldn't… JD pushed himself forward, till he stood side by side with Tom. Milly was on the floor, fighting against the force that had hold of her limbs, blood all over her face and neck. Tom too was bleeding from a wound on his wrist. A circular shape that cut through the protective tattoos.

"No!" JD screamed as he realized what Tom had done, what Tom was doing. He had inscribed himself with the mark of Tezcatlipoca, signing the contract that offered up his own body for the god to possess.

The dark cloud released Milly and she collapsed on the floor, coughing and gasping for air. It took shape once more, forming into the figure of a huge man, with glowing silver eyes. It moved towards Tom, hands reaching for his face, stroking his skin, down his neck, shoulder and towards the mark Tom had carved into his own arm. Tendrils of smoke curled around the symbol and JD saw them creep under Tom's skin, like worms burying under flesh.

Tom turned to JD. Tears cut a track through the dirt and blood on his face.

"Ready?" Tom said, as he closed his eyes and stretched out his arms.

Ready? JD thought. Tom couldn't possibly mean what he thought he meant. In offering up his body to the god he was setting a trap. But triggering it would mean killing Tom and there was no way JD could kill his best friend. Whereas Milly had fought the demon god off, Tom was welcoming it in. It would possess him any moment and then it would all be over. There had to be some way to stop the god. A way to break the contract Tom had just so stupidly, so selflessly, signed.

The veins on Tom's arm turned black, as the shadow god

seeped into his bloodstream. JD had only a matter of seconds before it would be over. He knew what he had to do. He couldn't let the demon god take Tom's body, even if it meant doing the unthinkable. There was only one choice.

He swung his blade, bringing it down on his friend. Tom cried out in agony and fell, first to his knees and then toppling over. He lay in a growing pool of blood, his eyes wide open. But he was alive. JD hadn't taken his life. He had taken his hand.

JD had sliced it off just below the elbow, cutting away the symbol that had given the demon permission to take him. JD swiped off his belt and wrapped it around Tom's arm, yanking it tight.

The shadow god threw its head back and roared, a sound like thunder that shook the pyramid, and turned relentlessly back towards Milly. But as dark clouds swirled on the horizon, a bead of golden sunlight broke through. Dawn was coming.

The sky turned a pale pink, then orange as the sun rose on the first day of the equinox. Beams of golden light spread across the land below like spears heading straight for the pyramid. Tezcatlipoca screeched as the first shard of light struck him, backing away, trying to creep into the darkness within the pyramid, but there was no escaping the sun or the god it represented. Quetzalcoatl had come to reclaim his temple.

"The blade," JD said, remembering that now was their chance to destroy it for ever.

It lay on the floor by Tom's side. JD clutched it up and scrambled to the very centre of the platform, but then, for a split second, he hesitated. This blade was a key that could open a gateway to the Netherworld. This could be the chance he had been looking for to take the fight to the demons and end their attacks on the human world once and for all.

He looked at Tom, pale and bleeding. The twins and Connor were scattered on the steps below, battered and bruised. They weren't ready. They might never be ready. The blade had to be destroyed.

He raised it above his head, offering it up to the sky. A ray of sunlight hit the blade and refracted like light on a disco ball. Everywhere the light touched was basked in gold. The bodies of Zyanya and her Jaguar Warriors turned to dust under its power. The cloud of swirling darkness – all that was left of Tezcatlipoca – blasted apart. The light grew brighter and brighter till JD had to close his eyes.

When he dared open them again, everything was still and his hand was empty. The blade was gone and the only sign that Tezcatlipoca had ever tried to return was a scorch mark on the ground in the shape of a man. Zek, Niv and Connor clambered up the final steps to join them on the platform. They were hurt, but they were alive.

JD turned back to Tom, who sat propped up against the altar. He was pale, terrifyingly so, with blue-tinged lips and dark circles around his eyes. It reminded JD of that time they'd played a concert on Halloween and all had skulls painted on their faces. Tom hadn't wanted to clean his off.

Milly was by Tom's side. She tore a strip off her robe and tied it around Tom's arm, stemming the blood.

"What did you do that for?" she snapped.

"To save him," JD said, coming to kneel beside his friend.

"Pretty drastic move, mate," Tom said weakly.

"Pretty drastic situation." JD looked at Tom's arm. The tourniquet had slowed the blood loss but Milly's makeshift bandage was already soaked through. He met her gaze. He might have acted quickly enough to save Tom's soul, but had he cost him his life in the process?

Milly stroked Tom's forehead with a shaking hand. "I meant you anyway, you idiot," she said. "That was so stupid. You could have been killed."

"Well," Tom said, "I couldn't lose you yet. We were only just getting to know each other."

Milly wiped a tear away from her cheek and leaned in to place a kiss on Tom's lips. When she straightened, Tom's eyes were closed. "Is he...?" she said, horrified.

"Just passed out," JD said, checking Tom's pulse. "But we need to get him to a hospital and fast."

Connor kneeled down and scooped the unconscious

Tom up in his strong arms. "That must have been quite some kiss, Milly," he said, forcing a smile.

Rain started to fall as the storm clouds above gave up the fight.

"Come on," JD said. "Let's get out of here."

Stay

Milly waited outside the hospital room, watching the boys through the glass. The doctor had said they'd been unable to reattach the hand. Tom had lost a lot of blood and would need to be kept under observation for a few days. But he would live.

Tom was propped up against three white pillows while Connor fussed around him. Zek seemed to be flicking through all the channels on the small TV attached to the wall, while Niv played with the buttons on Tom's bed. JD stood in the far corner, not joining in. Milly could see her own guilt reflected back on his drawn face. Tom had nearly died to save her. She looked down at the bleached lino floor and wanted it to swallow her up. All of this, all of this pain, had been to protect her.

"So, you've got to the self-pity phase?"

Milly looked up to see Gail standing over her, carrying

two cups of steaming coffee. She was dressed in a hospital gown and moved without her usual grace.

"Gail." Milly stood up and tried to hug Gail, made difficult by the coffee. "They told me you'd been hurt."

Gail placed the coffees on a small side table and gave Milly a proper hug. "I'm okay. We're all okay." Gail let her go.

"But Tom's hand… I…" Milly choked back tears.

Gail sat down in a blue plastic seat with her leg outstretched. "Having a disability doesn't make him weak. I should know." She tapped her eyepatch. Milly realized she had never asked anyone what happened to Gail.

"Was that a demon too?"

Gail drummed her fingers against the side of her coffee cup. "You know I was in a band, back in the day? An all-girl rock band, and we were good; we could have been great even…had it not been for the demon. We were filming a video in a graveyard in Norway when it attacked. It killed my friends. My girlfriend."

"Oh, I'm so sorry."

"Don't worry. I got my own back. I smashed its head in with a spade. But not before it had clawed out my eye and shattered the bones in my leg."

"You're badass, Gail."

"Back then I wasn't. I was just a messed-up girl who'd watched her friends die. No one believed me, of course. A black teenager trying to tell the authorities the truth? It got me locked up in a psychiatric hospital for three years." She tapped the silver tip of her cane to her temple.

Milly wasn't surprised. She imagined what would happen if she tried to tell anyone about what she'd been through over the past week. They'd probably try and lock her up too. "I'm so sorry, that must have been terrible."

"You know the worst thing? I almost believed them. I almost believed that I had imagined it all. It got so bad that I almost thought about..." Gail didn't need to finish. "I bought my way out of there, but it took all the money I had left from the band. Everything I had in the world, gone like that." She clapped her hands together. "After that, I wandered around the world, trying to work out what I was supposed to do with my life. That night, when I found Tom," Gail said, a sad smile creasing her cheeks, "crying over the body of his mother, it didn't just save his life, it saved mine. I knew then what I had to do. Hit back."

"Tom was the first?"

Gail nodded. "I thought it was enough, just to protect that one boy. But then along came JD, the twins and finally Connor."

"So you put the band together?"

"I didn't know at first that we would be a band. At first, I thought it was just about giving the boys a home. But when I heard Tom playing the piano, I knew. If we were going to fight, if we were going to make a difference, we needed money. Starting the band seemed the obvious solution."

"It doesn't seem right," Milly said. "That you should have to fight this battle alone. If only you could tell people…"

"Sometimes keeping people in the dark is the best way to keep them safe," Gail said. "Maybe one day the world will be ready to know. But for now, we just get on with the job."

The job, Milly thought. If only she had something like that to keep her going. They watched hospital life move around them. Nurses and doctors rushing about. They had a purpose. What did Milly have?

"So, what are your plans?" Gail asked, ignoring the unsubtle whispers of a woman sitting on the other side of the corridor. The woman had clearly recognized Gail and was doing a bad job of pretending she hadn't.

Milly joined in the pretence, blocking the woman out. "To be honest, I don't have a clue. My mother called all the shots in our life. So now…" She trailed off, and stared at an old man hobbling past using a Zimmer frame. The truth was, Milly knew exactly what she wanted to do. The idea had started to itch away at her the day she and the boys had written that song together. Even being kidnapped and nearly killed hadn't dissuaded her: she wanted to do what Slay did. She wanted to make music and fight evil. But she knew it was a useless desire. It was clear from the start that they'd never wanted her around.

"He kicked us out." Milly turned to see Zek and the others

piling out of Tom's room. "Can you believe it? Apparently we weren't helping."

"He needs rest, which he wasn't getting with you two pushing every button in the place," Connor said.

Niv drew a cross on his shoulder with his thumb.

"What did you call me?" Connor said, ready for a fight.

"He called you a nurse," Milly translated.

"Oh, well, in that case." Connor scooped Niv up in a hug. Clearly nearly losing Tom was making him even more emotional than usual.

"Gail said you will be leaving us?" Zek said, without meeting Milly's eyes.

"My flight back to Chicago leaves in a couple of hours," Milly said. She'd have to go back and sort out her mother's estate. Sell the house maybe. She didn't know where to begin, but she knew there was no point in dragging this out any longer.

You must? Niv signed one-handed, his other hand trapped by Connor's hug.

"I've caused you lot enough trouble."

"Not trouble," Connor said, letting go of Niv. "It's been fun."

"You have a very unique idea of fun, Con," Milly said.

"We'll…you know." Connor's words caught in his throat.

"Yeah," Milly said. "I know."

Connor wrapped her up in a hug too. She winced at the

pain in her chest. The doctors had seen to her wound too. It would heal, but leave a nasty scar.

"Sorry," Connor said, loosening his grip but not letting her go. Zek and then Niv joined him. She stayed there, wrapped in the safety of their arms, fighting back the tears. When they finally let her go, she struggled out a smile.

Stay in contact, Niv signed.

Promise, she answered.

Connor and the twins wandered away, leaving JD behind them. The idea of watching him go was almost too much for Milly. He looked down at his feet, as if he too was struggling to look at her.

"So," she said, finally breaking the awkward silence between them. "I never got the chance to thank you for saving me."

"That's okay, just doing our jobs. I guess I never got the chance to thank you for saving me back."

Milly hesitated, rocking forward on her feet. JD always felt so distant, so unreachable. They stood barely a metre apart and yet it felt like miles. Even after everything they'd been through, reaching out to JD now felt like too big a risk to take. He finally looked up and they stared into each other's eyes, both frozen.

"Well," she said at last. "Take care of yourself."

JD nodded, as if respecting her decision. "You too."

"I'll see you back at the hotel," Gail said. Milly had almost forgotten the woman was still there. "Once I make them sign my discharge forms. Honestly, so much fuss for a few scratches."

"You lost a pint of blood, Gail," JD said.

"*Pfff.*" Gail waved away his concern. "You're as bad as the nurses. It was half a pint, tops."

"You should ask if you can keep the gown," JD said. "It looks good on you." He dodged the swing of Gail's cane and turned to leave, before remembering something. "Tom wants to talk to you, Milly." He gestured over his shoulder at Tom's room. And with that, he left, his trainers squeaking on the bleached floors.

Milly looked at Tom lying in the bed. He looked so small and frail amid all the white pillows.

"Go on," Gail said. "You've got plenty of time before your flight."

Milly knocked gently on the door before entering.

Tom's pale face broke into a huge grin on seeing her. "Milly!" He reached out his hand.

Milly crossed the gap between them in a single, quick stride and took it. It was so warm. Tom shifted over and patted the space on the side of his bed. Milly perched on the edge, careful not to shake the bed too much.

"So," Tom said, rubbing his thumb in circles on the back of Milly's hand. "I wanted to ask you something."

Milly couldn't face it. "My flight is leaving in a couple of hours."

"About that." Milly looked from his sparkling green eyes to the cupid bow of his lips. She'd kissed him when she thought she was losing him; would she ever be that brave again? Tom smiled. "Stay."

Butterflies did swan dives in her stomach. Was he really saying what she thought he was?

"But…there's no place for me."

"Well, Slay need a new pianist." It took a while for Milly to understand what Tom meant. Then she looked at his bandages.

"No, Tom, you'll be okay. They can do amazing things with prosthetics, you'll be—"

Tom stopped her by squeezing her hand. "It's not that, Milly. I mean, yes, it is that. Sure, maybe I can play a bit with one hand, or Zek is very excited about me getting a cyber hand. But it's more than that. I can't risk it."

"Risk what?"

"The fame."

Milly shook her head, confused.

"When Tezcatlipoca tried to possess me, I felt it. That hunger for power. I would do anything for it. And I can still feel it now, Milly." He squeezed her hand again. "It scares me. I wanted it so badly, I still want it. It reminded me of my mother – willing to do anything just to be adored again. Gail warned us all about what fame can do to people, how the power can twist them, turn them evil. That unless you approach it with a pure heart, it can grip you. And my heart, Milly—"

"No, Tom, no," Milly said, laying her hand on his chest. "You're the kindest, purest person I have ever known."

"And I want to believe that. I want to hold onto that side of me – so don't you see? I can't do it any more. I can't be onstage, I can't be in the spotlight."

"But he tried to possess me too, Tom. How do you know it won't do the same to me?"

"Answer me this: have you ever, once in your life, wanted to be famous?"

Milly thought about that. Her whole life she'd seen her mother chasing fame and fortune, seen how it had made her ruthless and cold.

"No," she said. "No, I haven't."

"And that is why you will be okay. And maybe I will be too, one day, when I can trust myself again. But till then, I need you. It's why we all need you."

Milly could feel his heart beat beneath her hand. Could she do this?

"Okay," she said. "Just until you're better."

"It's not easy, this life, you know that, right? And I'm not just talking about…" He looked around to make sure no one outside could overhear. "Going up against demons every week. I mean being on the road, the lack of privacy. It's a lot to handle. It's selfish of me to even suggest it." Tom shook his head, as if he regretted asking.

"It's not. It's what I want. My whole life I've just wanted to belong. I was always on the outside looking in. But since meeting you and the others, it's like…it's like someone finally sees me. The real me. Or if not the real me, then the me I want to be. I'm not making any sense." She looked down at her hands.

Tom laid his hand on her face. "You're making perfect sense."

Milly looked down as their fingers tentatively entwined. "How much do you remember? From the pyramid?"

"I remember when JD cut my arm off. Kind of hard to forget."

"And…after that?"

"Oh, you mean when you kissed me?" Tom grinned.

Milly felt her cheeks flush. She'd part hoped that he hadn't remembered it. "It was…I mean…I thought you were dying."

"Well, I hope I don't have to nearly die for you to kiss me again."

Milly bit down on her lip, holding back the smile that was threatening to give her away.

She leaned gently towards him. His hand ran up her arm to her neck, his fingers brushing the back of her hair. The centimetres between them melted away. Her lips parted.

"Ahem."

Milly jumped back so fast she nearly fell off the bed.

"Gail!" Tom said, leaning back into his pillow. "Hi."

Gail looked between the two of them, her lips pursed, eyebrow raised. "Hi yourself."

"Milly and I were just, um, discussing her joining the band."

"Sure," Gail said, her expression softening slightly. "And what conclusion did you come to?"

They both looked at Milly. "If you're okay with it?"

"I am very much okay with it," Gail said. "And the boys will be too. Once they get used to the idea. Welcome to Slay."

Milly stood and wrapped her arms around Gail's neck. "Thank you," she whispered.

"You're home now," Gail replied.

Back to business

JD and the others were driven to a hotel in Cancún by an overly chatty taxi driver in reflective sunglasses. JD ignored him. He really needed some headspace to organize his thoughts – the feeling of guilt over what he'd done to Tom and the wrenching emptiness he felt at having said goodbye to Milly.

Zek stopped him as they exited the lift which opened into their suite, letting the other two go ahead. "Do you want to talk about it?"

JD shook his head.

"Well, thank God for that."

JD smiled, appreciating his friend's attempt at humour. Zek winked as he passed, letting JD know that despite all the bravado, he was there for him. He was always there.

Inside the suite, Connor and Zek ran around, putting dibs on the best room. Niv walked into the kitchenette and pulled out two cans of cola from a minibar. He threw one to JD, who caught it and collapsed onto a sofa, his tired muscles sinking into the soft cushions. As hotel suites went, this was one of the good ones. Three rooms led off the shared living space, and the view of the sea was spectacular.

"No fair!" Connor shouted, from one of the rooms. "Yours has a bath!"

"When was the last time you had a bath, Con?" Zek said, strolling out of his room, a fluffy white dressing gown wrapped over his jeans and T-shirt.

"Well, it would be nice to have the choice." Connor vaulted onto the sofa next to JD and pulled his sticks out of his back pocket.

Zek knocked Connor's baseball cap off as he passed, sliding into an armchair. Connor seemed too tired to even respond, and just put the cap back on.

"So, I guess Milly will be at the airport now," Zek said.

"I guess," JD said quietly.

"Shame," Zek said. "I was getting used to her."

"Me too," Connor said, opening a can of cashew nuts. "Remind me why she can't stay again?"

"It's not safe for her," JD said. It was a poor excuse and no one was buying it.

Zek snorted his disagreement. Niv held his index and little finger out like the horns of a bull and with his other hand made an explosive gesture as if the bull was relieving itself.

"She's not the same as us," JD replied, understanding Niv's gestures without needing his brother to translate.

"She kind of is, JD," Connor said. "Orphaned by demons. All alone in the world."

"And you have to admit, she can play piano," Zek said.

"It's too late now, anyway. She wanted to go home and who can blame her? I mean, who would want this life?" He held his hands up, indicating the hotel room.

"True enough," Zek said, throwing his legs over the arm of his chair. "She'd have to put up with Connor's snoring for a start."

"For the last time: I do not snore," Connor said.

Niv made small circles in front of his nose with his fist. Zek snorted with laughter.

"What'd he say?" Connor asked.

"He said you sound like a pig."

"Ah, shut up, the lot of you." He threw a cashew at Niv's head.

The elevator rumbled and pinged. Gail was back. And she wasn't alone. JD's heart skipped when he realized who was with her.

"Hi," Milly said with a small wave.

Connor was the first to jump up. "Does this mean…?" He looked at Gail, a hopeful smile on his face.

"Milly will be taking Tom's place while he recuperates, as long as that's okay with everyone."

"Yes!" Connor said, giving Milly an enthusiastic high five.

"Very okay," Zek said, kissing Milly on her right cheek. Niv did the same to Milly's left, and she squirmed, squeezed between the twins.

"Thanks," she said, before looking over at JD.

What could he say? That he was so glad to see her he could hardly find the words? "Welcome aboard," he said at last. Milly's smile made his heart ache.

"Um, one thing," Zek said, raising a finger in the air. "We are a boy band, right?"

"We are that," Connor agreed.

"And Milly is, well, I hate to break this to you, Milly, but you are not a boy."

"Is that a problem?" Milly said.

"Hmm," Gail said, stroking her chin and looking Milly up and down. "The fans might not like it."

"Simple," Connor said. He yanked a hoodie out of his bag and pulled it over Milly's head. It swamped her. "Finishing touch." He lifted the cap off his head and placed it on Milly's, where it fell to cover her eyes.

"That could work," Gail said, stepping back to consider Milly's new look.

"It might be hard to hide. Although, I must say, Milly, you do make a very good boy," Zek said.

"Rock stars have hidden bigger secrets, believe you me," Gail said, adjusting Connor's cap and tucking Milly's hair up under it. "I'll draft the press release tomorrow announcing that… I guess you'll need a new name."

"Ooh, ooh," Connor said excitedly, "let me pick." He sat down on the sofa and considered Milly, stroking his chin in serious thought. "Um, Frank. No, Fred. No. Frederick."

"How about Milo?" JD said. "Then we can just call you Mils."

Milly smiled softly and took a seat next to him. "Works for me."

JD looked from Milly to Connor and the twins, who were both smiling, and something struck him. It didn't feel weird. It was as if Milly was always meant to be a part of their strange family.

"So," said Gail, clapping her hands together and leaning against the breakfast bar. "Back to business."

"Can we go after the lizard men now?" Connor said, leaping back onto the sofa.

"Will you stop it with your lizard men?" Zek said.

"Come on, guys. Why will none of you believe me? After all we've seen. You believe me, don't you, Niv?"

Niv stretched out his flat hand. He waved it from side to side. *Maybe.*

"Are you seriously trying to make us believe that lizard men have taken over Hollywood?" Zek said.

"He might be onto something there," Milly said quietly. "I mean, take LA. It's hot, like, all the time. Lizards like the heat."

"See!' Connor said triumphantly. "And lizards only have three-minute memories. It would explain all those Hollywood remakes, right?"

"That's goldfish, Connor. Goldfish," said Zek. "Maybe everyone in Hollywood has been taken over by goldfish?"

Despite himself, JD laughed at Zek's puckered lips.

"We'll check out your lizard men another time, Connor, okay?" Gail said, after Connor threw another cashew nut at Zek's head. "A friend has been in touch and she needs some help with a pretty nasty demon that has been terrorizing the area for years."

"Where?" JD said. Nothing could take his mind off his feelings like the prospect of kicking some demon butt.

"Japan."

Zek caught a flying cashew and popped it into his mouth. "We've never played Japan before, have we?"

JD put his hands behind his head and leaned back in on the sofa. "Then I guess it's time we did."

SLAY 2

SLAY are BACK for a second kick-ass adventure...
And this time they're heading to Tokyo.

Join Milly, JD, Tom, Connor, Niv and Zek for
more music-playing, demon-slaying,
hell-raising fun!

COMING SOON

A note from Kim

In 2012, I spent four months travelling in Central America exploring Aztec and Mayan temples, many only recently excavated. The temple that appears in *SLAY* is a fictional amalgamation of many of the ones I visited. I have taken a few liberties in regard to Aztec rituals, although the Toxcatl Massacre was a true and tragic event.